The
ROYAL ROAD
to the
STARS

The
ROYAL ROAD
to the
STARS

Colin Barker

Matador
9 Priory Business Park,
Wistow Road, Kibworth Beauchamp,
Leicestershire, LE8 0RX
Tel: 0116 279 2299
Email: books@troubador.co.uk
Web: www.troubador.co.uk/matador
Twitter: @matadorbooks

ISBN: 978 1800461 024

British Library Cataloguing in Publication Data.
A catalogue record for this book is available from the British Library.

Printed and bound by CPI Group (UK) Ltd, Croydon, CR0 4YY
Typeset in 11pt Minion Pro by Troubador Publishing Ltd, Leicester, UK

Matador is an imprint of Troubador Publishing Ltd

To Carel and Dan

'Dreams are the Royal Road...'
Sigmund Freud. 1900

'Here we are all, by day; by night we're hurled
By dreams, each one, into a several world.'
Robert Herrick (1591–1674)

'across the gulfs of space.... intellects vast and cool and
unsympathetic.... regarded earth....'
The War of The Worlds, H.G.Wells. 1898

PROLOGUE

'The Royal Road to the Stars' is the story of Oliver and Pierre, a man and a dog, chosen to tackle the greatest earthly journey ever made. One whose aim was no less than securing the future of humanity. But when Oliver took the first step to start this walk of a thousand miles, he had no hint of the distance he must travel, the wonders he would see, or the sufferings he must endure.

But what had led to this unsought odyssey? Basically, man's fear of alien judgement had come true: earthly affairs, at last, had provoked the scrutiny of extra-terrestrials. But not with any sort of envy; more a stern appraisal, with the power to assess mankind's fitness to influence the planet's future.

The journey began with Oliver and his brother Frank rescuing Pierre, an abandoned puppy, thinking little of the significance of this kind act. How could they have possibly known where that would lead them? They had no way of looking into the 'seeds of time' to know which grain would grow, nor could they have even dreamt that, far from Earth, decisions that would shape its future had already been made. There would have been no inkling that the arrival of Pierre would precipitate the crisis facing mankind, or trigger the awakening of dormant allies in the ensuing cosmic drama. But it was soon made clear to the brothers that here was no ordinary puppy. And in their local pub, the Lamb and Limpet, soon after the rescue, they were discussing a surprising discovery about the little animal, who was to play such a crucial role in what was to come.

1

It all began when the conference on the south coast that Frank and his brother Oliver had attended finished early. And as it was a lovely sunny June day, they decided to leave the main trunk road and take a more leisurely route home, through country lanes, across the lovely High Weald of Kent.

At one point where the wooded view lay spread out before them, they pulled into a scenic lay-by behind a black van to change drivers. The van pulled away almost at once, and near where it had been standing Frank saw something moving, like a tiny blind animal on the ground.

He approached it cautiously, but relaxed when he saw it was a tiny, feeble puppy. There was no possibility of recalling the van, and neither brother had any intention of leaving the little creature to fend for itself. And that was how Pierre, for that turned out to be his name, came into their lives and the journey began.

***

'Well, that's it then,' said Frank, pushing away his empty pint mug of 'Wreaker's Ruin'. 'You keep him at home tonight, and bring him round to us tomorrow. I'll tell Cynthia.'

'Be careful what you say to her,' said Oliver, 'it needs careful handling.'

Adrian Purvoice's ears pricked up, for the landlord of their local, phoney posh but shrewd, was listening to the Penrose brothers from behind the bar. Thrown together since the early death of their parents, sturdy Frank was the elder, with his unruly fair hair and broad good-natured face, unpretentious, tolerant and easygoing, a freelance engineering consultant much in demand. *Easy to underestimate*, *men like him*, Adrian mused, thinking of Frank's beautiful, bright wife, Cynthia. But Oliver, his brother, recently returned from Australia where he had been working for the last five months, was more of a mystery.

Beside his brother he looked delicate, which was misleading, and a boyhood accident, whilst in Frank's charge, had left him with a slight limp, which made him feel awkward. But behind the guarded manner and a natural reserve, he was intensely loyal to his brother, and made a good living playing the stock market. His acute intelligence, combined with a shy, vulnerable warmth, made him very attractive to all kinds of women. But he missed many chances, liking others to make the running in the first blush of a relationship, and although gentle in life, he could be less tender in love. He was not decisive like Frank, disliking having to make decisions, especially personal ones.

Later that evening, Frank suggested to his wife, Cynthia, that they might get a puppy. 'How could you even think of such a thing,' she cried, 'with dear Pommard still so alive, in my thoughts!'

'The poodle died six months ago,' said Frank. 'We must move on.'

'If you'd cared for him, you wouldn't say that!' she cried.

'What could be more helpful in overcoming your grief than a rescue puppy?' Frank persisted, adding that he believed Oliver was coming around with just such a canine delight that evening.

Cynthia wondered who would be responsible for this 'irresistible animal'.

'No problem,' said Frank, 'he can sleep in the summerhouse, and I'll take him for walks. He'll like that.'

'It won't do,' she said. 'Tell Oliver to take the animal back to where it came from.'

'No can do,' said Frank, 'we found him abandoned in a lay-by when we were driving back from the south coast.'

'That's sad, but far better to take it to a vet who'll find it a good home.'

***

The following evening after supper, the doorbell rang and Frank quickly left the room. Oliver was waiting outside the front door, holding in his arms a folded blanket, from which a small furry face peeped out.

'How did you get on?' he whispered.

'You're to take it away,' said Frank.

'Women can be hard about such things,' said Oliver. 'You didn't mention…?'

'No, of course not.'

'We'll have to tell her,' said Oliver. 'Look, I can't stand here forever, holding this… animal, so let's just get it over with.'

'Animal!' said the puppy. 'Tired of 'cute little fellow', are we?"

'No, but please, *please* don't say anything when you meet Cynthia,' said Oliver. 'Just wait quietly, and then *calmly* release your inner waif.'

'And keep it *simple,*' added Frank.

'I'm a gifted canine, not a parrot.'

'It's for your own good,' said Frank, 'you'll see.'

'Is there a *toilette* in there?' the puppy asked, hopefully.

They carried him into the kitchen, where Cynthia had been painting her toenails. Frank put him on the floor and he ran over, sniffed at her foot, looked puzzled and sneezed. Which, given his urgent need, was unfortunate.

'Why don't we leave you two alone?' said Frank, looking meaningfully at Oliver, and gently urging the puppy forward with his foot. They left the room, and their little charge sat down and looked up at Cynthia appealingly. He then jumped up, leaving another small token on the floor.

4

'You need a pee,' she said, using an odd voice. 'There's a cat-flap in the door behind you. Please use it, and do what you need to do in the garden.'

'*Mon dieu,* you speak *Canine,*' said the puppy in surprise, sitting up, rather too abruptly.

'I'll '*mon dieu*' you, if you don't use that cat-flap,' Cynthia replied.

When he returned, she lifted him up, looked into his face and sniffed. 'I thought so,' she said in English, 'you reek of garlic – you're French.'

'*Non, non, Madame,*' said the puppy, wriggling uneasily in her grasp. 'No, no, I mean, British to the core. Rule Britannia. God save the Queen.'

'And you've slipped over the Channel illegally, I'll bet,' said Cynthia.

'Channel?' said the puppy. 'What is this Channel?'

Cynthia had had enough of this, and enquired if he knew the English word 'quarantine'. When he looked blank, she explained that, reflecting its length as a word, it referred to a long time behind bars. But then, seeing how sweet he was, and how crestfallen he'd become, she said softly, 'My dear, what is your name?'

'Pierre, *Madame,*' said the puppy.

'Stay here if you like, I don't care,' said Cynthia. 'You can use Cain's cat-flap. As you know, there's plenty of room for you to get in and out.'

Pierre paused, and then said, in a small voice, 'Is your cat *large*?'

'Cain's pretty big,' said Cynthia, after a moment's thought, 'shoulders on him like a Sumo wrestler – even got jammed in the old cat-flap once. But if you wished to live with us, you'd be welcome to share his food – I don't think he'd mind, what with the number of rats he gets through. I expect you saw the remains of dead rodents when you were in the garden.'

'I did seem to be in some kind of animal *cimetiere*,' said Pierre.

'Disgusting, isn't it?' said Cynthia. 'We call it the 'feline killing fields'. We complain about it, but he doesn't listen. Perhaps you could have a word with his highness and ask him to show some restraint?'

'If only I could, dear lady.'

'Don't you animals have an unspoken bond about such things?'

'*Madame*,' said little Pierre with dignity, drawing himself up to his full height, 'even though I lack years, I am aware that inter-species communication has yet to achieve the harmony to which more refined animals aspire.'

'Well expressed,' said Cynthia, delighted with his eloquence.

'Now you must forgive me, *Madame*,' said Pierre, 'for I fear I'm trespassing unduly on your time.'

Cynthia, although disappointed, fully understood his sentiments about staying, and proposed an alternative. 'Molly, our neighbour, loves animals, and she would undoubtedly welcome you into her ménage. Would you care for an introduction?'

'And quarantine?' said Pierre, with a slight shudder.

'An English prison is hardly the place for a puppy of your sensibilities,' said Cynthia.

'Kindness itself of you to propose such a course of action,' said the puppy, 'but I find that I am unable to subdue a strong urge to move on.'

'As you wish,' Cynthia smiled.

'I will now dictate a note of thanks for your husband,' said Pierre, 'and if you'd be so good as to write it out for me, I'll be running along. I assume that the front gate is unlocked,' he added, 'and hope that *Monsieur* Cain will not see my hasty departure as a sign of rudeness. And now, *Madame*, if you've a pen and some paper handy…'

***

Pierre signed the note with a moist little paw, licked Cynthia on both cheeks and made a little bow. 'Goodbye, *Madame,*' he said. 'As I am rather small, perhaps you would set me down on the floor?'

Outside, his *savoir faire* faltered, for gallantry is tiring when you are tiny, even for a French-bred patrician puppy. He looked around the garden, but seeing nothing amiss, trotted down the path, pausing for a moment by the open garden gate. He carefully surveyed the dimly lighted street with its overhanging trees, and was about to step onto the pavement when a soft voice from the bushes flanking the path stopped him in his tracks.

The voice, feline, languorous and full of unspoken menace, came from the shadows. Pierre turned, and found himself facing a large tomcat standing on its hind legs, leaning against the wall and chewing. The shadow cast by the streetlight suggested he was wearing

7

a fedora, completing the illusion of a Chicago gangster. That meant nothing to the puppy, but he knew that he was in big trouble.

'Hey kid, what's the hurry?' said the big cat, moving lazily to block his path. 'Where's the fire?' He pronounced it 'da foire', which was confusing as well as frightening.

'Please excuse me, *Monsieur,*' said Pierre, 'but there is no 'foire' of which you speak, and you must pardon my haste, but I have far to go.'

'You sure punch above your weight with words, little one,' said the cat silkily. 'Overheard you talking to the human dame. Sounded *intimate* to me.' He pronounced the word with a slight Parisian intonation.

If he'd worn them, Pierre would have quaked in his boots, for here was no simple feline bruiser but an accomplished villain, and every instinct warned him to be careful. '*Monsieur*, I simply passed the time of day with the lady,' he stammered, 'and we parted with her good wishes for my future travels. Let me pass, I entreat you.'

'Let's get a better look at you, little froggie doggie,' said the cat, and stepped forward. In the pale light his dusty fur appeared deathly white, and the ravaged face beneath the ragged ears and the single eye confirmed that Jarvis, this lean and literate feline, was no stranger to bare-claw street fighting.

With the cat rearing high above him, Pierre shrank back, feebly wagging his little tail. A large dirty paw touched his cheek and he flinched, at which his tormentor laughed softly, and turning, said, 'See what we've got here.' In reply a rat- faced cat with bright malicious eyes limped out from the dark bushes, licking its lips with suggestive relish.

'Pick on someone your own size,' said a deep voice, and an enormous cat moved smoothly between Pierre and the two cats facing him. 'Vamoose, scratchings, before you get hurt,' it growled, making a lunge at the smaller cat, which leapt on top of a high fence surrounding the garden, throwing him a baleful glance before crashing away through the shrubbery.

'This young gentleman's under my protection,' the newcomer said to the remaining cat. 'Jarvis, I've warned you before to keep away and now...' He launched himself through the air, steel-tipped claws splayed and mouth open in a terrible grimace. His rival rolled onto his back and, paws flailing wildly, was dragged spitting and snarling into the bushes, where, after some muffled screams and choking gasps, all was silent.

The great cat pushed his way back through the undergrowth onto the path, shaking his head as if to clear it. 'Here no-one threatens those to whom my Mistress speaks,' he said. 'But forgive me, where are my manners? Pierre, is it not? Cain, at your service.'

Pierre bowed politely and said, '*L'honneur est entièrement mienne, Monsieur Cain.*'

'I fear my French is limited to pleasantries,' said the cat. 'Might we converse in English, that inter-species tongue familiar to animals of our rank?'

'By all means,' said Pierre.

Cain smiled, as far as his feline countenance and injuries permitted, and said, 'I understand you are seeking accommodation alternative to that offered you?' Pierre replied that he feared a stay on a protracted basis would incommode Cain, for there was mention of sharing his food, which he felt, as would all well-bred animals, constituted a grave breach of etiquette.

'This country!' said Cain. 'Unlike in France, here the food is scarcely 'prepared' for we animals. It arrives in cylindrical tin containers, with names too hideous to mention, which the English humans hack open with a vicious tool. Then the inedible slop inside them is thrown into a noxious utensil called a 'bowl', more suitable for the products of basic bodily functions than healthy food. This often remains on the floor long after its contents are palatable, or even wholesome.'

'*Mon dieu,*' muttered Pierre under his breath, his skin paling beneath his still scanty coat.

'And thus I find myself compelled to consume rats,' said Cain, 'a taste not entirely repugnant to me, but monotonous when unseasoned or ungarnished.'

'*Sacré bleu,*' cried Pierre, 'and to think that this gastronomic desert will be my future home, for I am half English. My mother, born and bred in Chelsea, met my father at a diplomatic reception, when he was Chief of Canine Security to the French Embassy in South Kensington. An area perhaps familiar to you, Monsieur Cain?'

'Alas, only by repute, for I come from humbler stock than you, although were I to be described as '*haut bourgeois*' it would not be unduly immodest of me to agree,' said Cain, adding that others might also remark, without fear of rebuke, that his features betrayed an undeniable Maine Coon pedigree.

This was grown-up stuff, and Pierre began trembling from nervous exhaustion. Cain, detecting his discomposure, made a proposal. 'Permit me, my dear Pierre, to intercede with the mistress, to whom I will stress your need for sanctuary.'

He then offered Pierre a place to rest for the night, promising him his protection and an opportunity to talk further in the morning. And with that he led the way to a pleasant little summerhouse in the garden.

***

After making sure that Pierre was sleeping comfortably, Cain squeezed through the cat-flap in the kitchen, looked up at Cynthia sitting at the table and said, for the first time in English, 'Mistress, may I have a word?'

She recovered quickly from the shock. 'Of course,' she said, aware that *lingua fauna* etiquette would frown upon her reference to an animal's choice of language. Only in the final moment between predator and prey could the latter use any tongue it wished without offence. 'How can I help you, Cain?' she said, gesturing to a chair beside her.

The huge cat was in his prime, but lighter days were several hundred rats behind him, and the resultant payload influenced both launch and hard landing onto the chair. After a short pause, he said, 'May we discuss the plight of a small animal who recently had the pleasure of addressing you?'

'To whom do you refer?' said Cynthia.

'A mere puppy, introduced to you by your husband.'

'Oh, *Pierre*. We spoke briefly, but he politely declined my offer of accommodation and left. He's French, you know.'

'Only *half* French,' said Cain, 'and his better half, if I may put it like that, is English.' He added that, when they had first met, he was able to reassure Pierre of their protection by punishing a local offender who was threatening him.

Cynthia glanced sharply at him. 'I suppose that means some poor creature is lying somewhere, licking its wounds,' she sighed. 'Where is the puppy now?'

'In the summerhouse.'

'I'll get a blanket for him and he can sleep in here. Is that all right with you, monster?'

'May I suggest, Mistress, that we leave him where he is at present, for he was sleeping comfortably when I left him.'

'Very well,' said Cynthia wearily. 'I suppose you are off now to delight the local kitties with your attention.'

'Whilst sampling the night air I may look in on a friend or two,' said Cain, coldly, 'or I may continue with my novel: 'A Cat of Nine Tales'. Sadly neglected of late, owing to my need to obtain murine supplements to a severely unbalanced diet. Goodnight, Mistress.'

***

Cain left the scene of his victory, but a little later the brothers, returning from the pub, saw evidence of the encounter on the garden path. Frank stared aghast at the scattered leaves and bloodstains, and Oliver pushed aside some foliage to reveal the body of Jarvis. 'The mark of Cain,' he said, grimly.

'We'd better bury it, now,' said Frank. 'Drag it behind the beech tree while I get a spade, and don't let Cynthia see what you're doing.'

With the remains of Jarvis discreetly interred in a shallow grave, Oliver went home, Frank went to bed and Cynthia slept through it all. Pierre dozed fitfully in the summerhouse, among the paraphernalia required for afternoon tea in the garden, old tennis rackets and faded parasols, before falling into a deep sleep where he was in a delicatessen of infinite size, with an eternity in which to sample its delights.

But none of them would have slept quite so peacefully if they had known what lay ahead.

2

Jarvis's absence caused considerable anguish to the Penroses' newish neighbour, Molly Tether-Hedges, for he was the flag-cat of her feline flotilla and Hood, his faithful lieutenant. The sight of the latter slinking home alone at first shocked her, but when Jarvis also failed to return, her blood boiled

She was a youngish, shapely, handsome woman, intelligent and accomplished, with old money, breeding and good taste. She loved animals, investing the rest of her emotional capital on affairs with unsuitable men, one of whom had been Adrian, landlord of the Lamb and Limpet pub.

Adrian, real name Dudley Grudge, had begun his working life as a manual worker in a Burton Brewery, and had risen socially in pace with his southward migration. Now in his early fifties, his thinning grey hair, long and grease-free, was tied back in a neat bow, and his ruddy, blue-veined cheeks were adorned with lavish silver sideburns. His waistline, like his flat Midlands vowels, had rounded and mellowed, and with a brightly coloured kerchief knotted around his neck, he behaved like the very embodiment of a cheery Dickensian landlord.

But behind the geniality lurked a cunning and clever operator. He often used his lack of basic education to disarm and deceive others, but this mask of gullibility couldn't always disguise his considerable intelligence, obscure his organising skills or dull his keen eye for business. And he pursued women avidly to achieve the social status he craved, outmatching male rivals through artfully simulated sincerity, particularly effective with those embracing modern spirituality.

Intelligent women like Molly soon saw through him, but took him for what he was at his best high-octane, sexually charged and amusing company. But when he began suffering from strange black moods, she became uneasy and turned to her vet, Vivian, an old flame, for advice.

'How do the episodes take him?' he asked. 'I trust he doesn't abuse you?'

'Not so far,' she said, 'but it frightens me that he might. One minute he's quite normal, and then his eyes glaze over, and he starts shaking and staggering about with his hands over his ears, screaming nonsense.'

'Can you make out what he says?'

"Get away from me! Get away from me!' over and over again, before going into a sort of coma for a minute or two. And when he recovers and I try to help him, he gets morose and aggressive.'

'Have you suggested he should seek professional help?'

'When I do,' said Molly, 'he gets really abusive, storms at me, and then denies anything that's happened. What should I do?'

'Unless you're really serious about him, I'd end the relationship,' said Vivian. 'You can't help him, and he might harm you. Let me know if you think you might be in any sort of danger.'

So Molly turned down the temperature of her relationship with Adrian, but that only seemed to stimulate his desire for her. And although he never threatened violence towards her, his unsought contact was a constant concern to her.

Adrian's moods were a mystery even to those who knew him well. What no-one knew was that the dark episodes were becoming more frequent as he went deeper and deeper into occult practices and witchcraft rituals. The 'spiritually woken' ladies, who had aroused his interest in the first place, were merely tepid practitioners, but not him. He corresponded with the leaders of illegal sects, consulted proscribed texts, and carried out rituals shunned by all but the most obsessive followers of the dark arts. But he was very careful to conceal his involvement in such practices from all who knew him.

However, none of his acquaintances would have been surprised to learn that Adrian had seen a business opportunity, even in modern witchcraft. He'd noticed Molly's devotion to cats, and, through his contacts, had spotted the chance to provide modern 'woke' witches wishing to enhance their 'coven-cred,' by supplying them with a must-have cat familiar. A creature well known, so he said, to be a protection for the fledgling witch 'coming into new powers'. But it needed to *look* the part – any old moggie would not do. What they needed was a Brittany-born, black cat, ritual-ready and preferably groomed by Molly. However, unknown to her clients was how thoroughly she vetted them before they could apply for a well-adjusted animal. And to continue protecting the cats, her involvement with their training continued, even after her affair with Adrian had ended.

Molly was devoted to all of her cats and, in spite of solid evidence that Jarvis and Hood were vicious and mean, suspected that Cain might have had a paw in whatever had happened to them. It was well known locally that, when the cats met nocturnally, their vocal exchange was as hostile as it was discordant. She worked herself up so much that, later in the day, she strode to the Penroses' and rapped smartly on their back door.

'Hallo, Molly,' said Cynthia, opening the door.

'I expect you know why I'm here,' said her neighbour.

'I'm sorry, but I don't,' said Cynthia.

'You or your husband know exactly what happened to Jarvis,' Molly cried.

'Jarvis?' said Cynthia, aware that some people assumed that detailed knowledge of things important to them were widely shared.

'And that, that… creature up there was responsible,' Molly choked, pointing out of the window at Cain, calmly snoozing on a tree branch in the garden.

'Why do you think he might be involved?' Cynthia said, following her gaze. 'He's not an aggressive creature.'

'My dear,' said Molly, 'that creature is a mauler, a ruffian and a bad lot.'

'Come back this evening and we'll see if we can get to the bottom of this,' said Cynthia.

***

After a day of further anguish, Molly returned to find the brothers with Cynthia, and they sat down in the living room to discuss the matter.

'Molly, I'm so sorry but I misled you,' Cynthia began. 'Cain had a fight yesterday, with a local animal, and it might have been Jarvis.'

Molly stared at her. 'How do you know? He can't have *told* you!'

'Not in *words*, obviously,' said Cynthia, regretting having to lie, 'but he had slight injuries, as if he'd been in a scrap.'

'I hope Jarvie isn't lying alone somewhere, in pain,' quavered Molly, bowing her head and crying softly.

Cynthia squeezed her hand, and Frank coughed awkwardly. She looked across to the two men, neither of whom met her eye. 'Do either of you know anything about this?' she snapped.

'Us?' said Frank, looking uncomfortable.

'I'm not accusing anybody,' said Cynthia, 'but we must search for Jarvis. If he was in a road accident someone may have thrown him over the hedge.' At this, Molly gave a great cry of anguish.

'No need to involve you ladies,' said Frank, hastily, 'Oliver and I can go and look for him.'

Ignoring the offer, Cynthia and Molly brushed past him and scoured the front garden, but found no sign of a body. However, in the back garden, they saw that the ground beneath the big beech had been disturbed, and Molly fell on her knees, clawing at the earth with her bare hands. And there, clogged with bloodied dirt, a furry body lay exposed. Throwing back her head, she screamed, 'I *knew* it, I *knew* it!'

'I swear, I knew nothing about this,' said Cynthia, putting her arm around Molly, now rocking with grief, and keening like an Irish peasant woman.

'Well?' she said, eyes blazing, turning to Frank, who stood watching, speechless with guilt.

Oliver pushed Molly gently aside, bent over the makeshift grave and pulled the furry cadaver from the ground. 'A rat,' he said, 'only a rat. There are others here too, probably buried by Cain for later consumption.'

Molly opened her eyes and shuddered. 'Come on, everyone,' said Cynthia, 'let's go and have a drink.' And for the two women it was the beginning of a close friendship, cemented by their shared sadness at the discovery next day by Frank of Jarvis's tattered body in the road, apparently the victim of a hit and run incident. The body was quietly interred in a sack and buried in Molly's garden with appropriate solemnity. A discreet wake was held afterwards, where Molly had a chance to chat to Oliver for the first time now he had returned from his overseas assignment.

And, as if to put a seal on the whole business, Frank, returning home after the ceremony, saw Cain on a branch of a tree in the garden, quietly washing a muddy paw. He gave the great Maine Coon a quick smile, and for a moment he swore he saw the great cat smirk. But when he calmly continued his meticulous toilet, Frank, although sure of his guilt, smiled again at the thought of the premeditated cover-up. He was sure Cain was behind it, but was a *cat* capable of such forethought and planning?

Little did Frank suspect that, in spite of his apparent composure, Cain was becoming deeply uneasy, his feline indifference to events slipping from him like a silk bathrobe from a woman's shoulders before stepping into a pool. If he could have pinned down the feeling, and used human words, he would have said that he felt uncomfortably like a 'creature in waiting', but for what he didn't know. And whatever it was, he was powerless to prevent it happening or to predict its outcome.

The other thing that he felt strongly was a connection between these feelings and the arrival of Pierre. And what was becoming clear to him was that he must protect the puppy at all costs. Already he had come to his aid when he was threatened by Jarvis, and his swift action over the exhumation of the body had given them both an unblemished record in the eyes of the world. That gave him some confidence for the future, but he sensed real danger coming, and just *knew* both he and Pierre would be involved.

A part of him that he didn't understand was stirring, and he dimly sensed that Pierre would soon embark on a perilous journey with Oliver. But where it would take them and what dangers they would face, he didn't know. And although its purpose was as yet unclear to him, he was sure the stakes were high, and the consequences of failure unthinkable. So worried was he about the future that he quite lost his appetite. This greatly benefitted the local rat population, whose leaders, if they had the equipment to consider the matter, would have thought it a just punishment for his former dietetic excesses.

3

Several days later, watching Pierre chasing butterflies in the garden, Cain wondered why he felt so uneasy about him. Cats possess an all-encompassing self-interest, so why did he worry about a *dog,* even one as special as Pierre, whose arrival he felt was ordained? His behaviour was also concerning the Penroses.

'He never seems to stop growing,' Cynthia said, 'and he's so *boisterous.*'

'I agree, he's getting out of hand,' said Frank. 'What we must do is find him a good trainer.'

'Any ideas?' said Cynthia.

'How about Molly?'

'*Molly!* With her cats?'

'Why not?' said Frank. 'She's really good with animals.'

'Dear Molly,' said Cynthia. 'Did you think that up all by yourself, dear?'

'It came up when I was talking to Cain about the buried rats.'

'What did he say?'

"Rats,' he said, '…remind me."

'Dear Cain,' said Cynthia. 'It's not in cats' nature to come clean.'

'When I said we were thinking of training Pierre,' said Frank, 'he thought Molly would be good for him. And if he boarded with her, being with mature female cats might 'round off his sharp edges".

'I could ask her,' said Cynthia doubtfully. 'Of course, we'd pay for his board and lodging.'

Frank nodded. 'At least he'll be well fed,' he said, adding, 'just like he's used to at home,' for Cynthia had looked up sharply.

It turned out that Molly was happy to have Pierre on a trial basis, and Cynthia told Cain. He was delighted to hear that his idea had been adopted. 'I'll discuss it with him, 'bete-a-bete,'" he said. But when he did, Pierre was not happy.

'In case you haven't noticed it,' he shouted, 'I'm a dog! And you expect me to live with a litter of kittens!'

'It's for the best, trust me,' said Cain.

Cynthia enlisted Frank's help in making it work. She'd noticed that Molly had got on well with Oliver at Jarvis's wake, and what better way could there be of keeping an eye on Pierre than getting Oliver more involved in the scheme? She even subsidised the lubricant that Frank used to oil the wheels of his brother's agreement, and after several pints of Wreaker's Ruin, he agreed to help Molly. 'I hope she realises he's only a puppy,' he said, almost tearfully.

'I'm sure she does,' said Frank, 'she loves dogs. Like Cynthia – remember how she grieved over Pommard.'

Oliver winced as he recalled the poodle's body crushed beneath his motorbike's wheels, and the memorable discussion afterwards. 'He was already dead, lying there on the path, when I ran him over,' he said, 'with Cain smirking away in the bushes like the Cheshire Cat.'

When the pair reported back, Cynthia sensed Oliver's reluctance. 'You helped bring Pierre here in the first place,' she said briskly, 'so get on with it, or we'll get rid of him.' In truth, she'd no intention of doing any such a thing, for she was extremely fond of the huge puppy. But it was as well that she cloaked her real feelings, for had she seen the full nature of Pommard's injuries, she'd have realised how much felines resent rivals, and that even now discretion might be needed in airing her warm feelings for Pierre too loudly.

***

Molly insisted that Pierre should be properly examined before she took charge of him, and her vet friend Vivian agreed to see him the next afternoon. Molly asked Cynthia to come round and bring Pierre with her, and when they arrived she let Pierre out into the garden, where he amused himself trying to catch flies in his mouth by leaping round and round and barking furiously.

Then Vivian turned up, a burly, cheerful man, tweedy and hirsute, with broken veins on his weathered cheeks and wiry, close-cropped hair. He watched Pierre in the garden for a moment, and asked how old he was.

'He was a small puppy when we got him,' said Cynthia, 'and we've had him about six months. What do you make of him?'

'He's basically Newfoundland,' said Vivian, 'and there's some Belgian Shepherd in him. Beautiful dog, but difficult. I take it he plays up if he's left alone.'

'He destroys everything he can get his paws on,' said Cynthia.

'Separation anxiety, the curse of these dogs,' said Vivian. 'See that big, fine-looking cat watching him?'

'He's ours – a Maine Coon, called Cain.'

'I recognise the breed,' said Vivian. 'He seems to have bonded with Pierre. Leaving them together might help calm him down. What do you think, Molly?'

'If you think it would help,' she said, with a thin smile.

'Wonder how she'll take that,' said Frank to his wife later, at home.

What else could she say? thought Cynthia.

***

The weather had turned warm and Pierre, dozing in the summerhouse, said to Cain, 'Provence is like this all summer long, I heard.'

'I was in Nice once, on a teen-Coon exchange trip,' said Cain. 'Doggie poo heaven.'

'My father said the place was full of stuck-up poodles,' said Pierre, 'with pink bows round their necks.'

'Sounds like the odious Pommard, the dumb beast, who taught my mistress to speak *lingua fauna*, against every animal etiquette,' said Cain. 'Canine *and* Feline. And when I asked him why he did it, he said: 'Dunno really, I'm trivial, me.' A scouse poodle! Can you imagine it?'

'Wasn't he run over?'

'In a way. Happily I was there to help my dear mistress over her grief at his death. 'What should I have done without you, dearest Cain?' she said, her very words.'

'Do you know a lot of the animals around here?' Pierre asked.

'I used to, but now I only know Madame Molly's older lady cats,' said Cain. 'They're from Brittany, and help train the kittens to be witches' familiars. Do you know anything about that?'

'No,' said Pierre.

'When her friend Adrian became involved in the occult,' Cain said, 'he got her to agree to train cats as 'familiars' – magical companions for witches. He then got on to some spiritual networks, floated the idea, and got a response from an ancient, underground spiritual Order based in Carnac in Brittany. Amongst other things, they'd traditionally bred cats to be familiars.'

'Were they an *evil* Order?' whispered Pierre.

'Not at all,' said Cain. 'Before providing Adrian with kittens they insisted that their cats must only be supplied to *white* magic practitioners, and they would only accept an instructor who was mature and skilled, with the kittens' welfare at heart. Two of their very spiritually advanced cats were to help with the training, and they would accompany consignments

26

of kittens bound for England. And there was another condition.'

'Go on,' said Pierre, sensing something coming.

'On one journey, another animal on an important mission had to be allowed to travel with the kittens.'

'What happened next?' said Pierre.

'Molly went to France,' said Cain, 'and was accepted by the Order, who trained her and provided two senior cats to help her. They were called Yvonne and Yvette. Molly then returned to England, and when enough kittens were ready, the Order hired a self-drive van to bring them over. They provided a driver who was to also take a puppy along with the kittens.'

'Don't tell me that was me,' said Pierre, in a quiet voice.

'It was,' said Cain, 'and it was no accident that the driver was told to leave you in the lay-by to be rescued by Frank and Oliver.'

Pierre gulped and looked forlorn, and it was then that Cain took the plunge. 'Pierre,' he said, 'I'm going to let you in on a great secret. Listen carefully.'

Pierre stared at him, startled by the serious tone of his voice.

'Something terrible is coming,' Cain said, 'I feel it in the air.' *Should he seek man's help?* he'd wondered, but like most cats, he regarded humans as slow-witted, clod-hopping meal tickets.

Pierre opened his mouth to speak but Cain went on. 'I speak of a change that may affect everything on Earth,' he said, 'deadly and dangerous. But I need more *facts.*'

27

'Facts?' said Pierre.

'Humans gather such things together when they meet something they don't understand.'

'Like when I'm barking to be let out?' said Pierre. 'They don't seem to understand that.'

'It's much more than that,' said Cain. 'They try to find *explanations* about what's happening. It helps them decide what to do next.'

'Really?' Pierre's eyes were wide with wonder. Animals were not designed to *analyse* phenomena, for life washed over them in great waves of uncertainty, which human scientists were only now discovering might be the true nature of reality.

Cain was in despair. Although Pierre was special, he was too young and not able to help him. He must look elsewhere and trust his instinct. 'Pierre,' he said, 'Molly's mature cats are wise as well as spiritual, and I must speak to them on this matter. They may feel as I do, and then we can decide what should be done.'

***

The opportunity for a meeting with the cats came when Frank took Pierre to stay with Molly. He sulked all the way to her house, and when they got there, Frank said, 'I know you're upset, but it won't be for long, and *please* don't say anything.'

Molly opened the door and smiled at Pierre. 'What a magnificent animal you're turning out to be,' she said, and his tail gave a tiny twitch. She let him out into the garden.

Frank said, 'He's a bit upset – we left without him seeing Oliver.'

'Ah, your brother,' said Molly, casually. 'Now he's back, I thought we might work together to help Pierre. I may have said as much to Cynthia.'

'He's very shy,' said Frank.

'Perhaps his wife or girlfriend might object to our meeting?' said Molly.

'No problem there,' laughed Frank. 'Incidentally, did Vivian mention Cain getting involved? If you'd rather he didn't…'

'He's welcome if it would help Pierre.'

'That's very kind of you, Molly,' said Frank. 'Do you think I might bring him around tomorrow?'

'The sooner the better,' said Molly. 'Perhaps I might mention it to your brother.'

'An excellent idea,' said Frank, smiling at her, ignoring a sudden pang of envy at his brother's good fortune.

***

In the pub that night Oliver mentioned receiving a telephone call from Molly. 'She's got this husky voice,' he said, 'and I'm to go around for a drink tomorrow.'

'Good,' grinned Frank, 'a nice person, and a very attractive woman into the bargain.'

'I don't want a bargain,' said Oliver.

'Women like her are rare,' said Frank.

'Not in my life, they're not,' said Oliver. But he would see Molly because his brother wanted it, and because it would help Pierre.

'How's our dear puppy?' Cynthia said when Frank came back.

Frank's mind, a powerful instrument of ice-cold reasoning, piercingly effective as an analytical tool, needed time to process the question. 'Molly told Oliver that it's a good time for Cain to help Pierre, who's going through a bad patch,' he said, 'and she asked me to take him around tomorrow.'

'I just hope it will help,' said Cynthia, disappointed, for she'd hoped for more exciting news.

***

Frank found Cain the next morning savouring a light rat snack under the beech tree. 'How can you eat that?' he said in disgust.

'A little *gritty*, but delicious nevertheless,' said Cain, licking his lips.

'Come with me, and help cheer Pierre up,' Frank said. 'And please, no English in front of Molly.'

'Delighted to help,' said Cain. 'Shall we walk together or would you prefer to carry me? If you choose the latter, you may find my breath rather *ratty* for your taste.'

'We'll walk,' said Frank, hurriedly. 'I'll ring Molly and see if she's ready for us. She has all those cats to look after.'

'Oh no, I hadn't forgotten *that*,' said Cain, with a smirk on his handsome features.

***

In the event it was early evening before Molly was free and Frank and Cain went to see her. The great cat stalked along the walls flanking the road and joined him at her doorstep.

'Do come in,' she said, glancing down at Cain, who ignored her and walked into the sitting room with a stiff back and vertical tail. 'Pierre's in the garden,' she said, 'tied up for a short while, I'm afraid, for refusing to eat at regular mealtimes.'

'How's he taking to the exercise?' said Frank.

'Another little problem,' said Molly. 'Magda agreed to take him for early morning jogs whilst she rode her bicycle.'

'Isn't she that rather thin, delicate-looking girl?' said Frank.

'Magda has a Nordic zeal for fitness and suffers from a slight eating disorder,' said Molly coldly, 'and is not, as you have observed, in robust health.'

'He must be a handful for someone like her,' said Frank.

Molly nodded coldly and said that her friend usually attached Pierre's lead to her bicycle's handlebars, and that the day before, whilst passing a tree, he had veered violently to the left, wrapping the lead around its trunk, dragging Magda after him. Propelled over the handlebars into a wet, nettle-filled ditch, she had suffered mild concussion, from which she had only partially recovered. Meanwhile Pierre had run away.

'Oh dear,' said Frank, afraid that he would burst out laughing. 'I hope he knows why he's being punished.'

'He knows exactly what he did,' said Molly. 'He came straight home and lay low, sulking.'

'Don't forget he's half French,' said Frank.

Meanwhile Cain had strolled over to where his friend was moodily chewing a sanitised rubber bone and spoke about his plan to contact Molly's cats in the outhouse.

'You must create a diversion,' he said.

'What is this word, 'diversion'?' asked Pierre.

Cats cannot grind their teeth but Cain managed a sound between a strangulated purr and a throatful of fur-balls. 'You know what I mean, you irritant,' he growled. 'Choke on something, make a racket, roll about in agony, just get them running to help you!'

'I could pretend I've been bitten by bees,' said Pierre thoughtfully.

'Wasps, hornets, giant spiders, I don't care,' muttered Cain. 'Just sound as if you're dying.'

'If I was on my back howling and rubbing at my nose with my paws, would that do?' said Pierre.

'Look,' said Cain, 'why don't I just stroll up to the cats' outhouse and hammer on the door? I'm not wasting any more time on you.'

'I'm going, I'm going,' said Pierre, and he ran off into the garden where he staggered, fell onto his back and clawed at his nose, uttering piercing screams. Frank and Molly ran to help, and Cain watched the drama for a moment before remembering its purpose. Then he slipped behind the wall of the cats' dwelling and disappeared inside.

Sensing the coast was clear Pierre, rolled over and

did some heavy-duty panting. 'Poor old fellow, you had us worried,' said Frank, on his knees beside him.

'Hmm. Nothing wrong with him that I can see,' said Molly.

'Well, he frightened old Cain away,' said Frank, looking around. 'Half-way home by now, I should think.' He then joined Molly walking back to the house, and a little later, after checking that Pierre was comfortable, they left to go to his house for a drink.

'I've spoken to Yvonne and Yvette, the two senior cats,' said Cain, emerging from the cats' home, and seeing that the coast was clear.

'What did they say?' said Pierre. 'Do they share your fears about the future?'

'Wait here and I'll get them,' he said, 'then they can tell you themselves.'

When Cain returned from the outhouse it was with two handsome black cats, who bowed to Pierre. '*Bonjour, Monsieur,*' they said in unison.

'Please tell me what is going on,' he said.

'Monsieur Cain's fears are shared by us and others,' said the one called Yvonne. 'The future is as yet unclear, but we feel that two great *affaires* lie ahead. One concerns the threat to man's dominant place on Earth, and to counter that there is a path that Monsieur Oliver and Pierre must tread. And on that journey they will meet the second issue: a great struggle between good and evil, which can only end in conflict.'

'I don't understand,' said Pierre. 'Why am I getting involved?'

'We don't know, but come with us now,' said Yvonne. 'We wish to show you somewhere where you may learn things that will be of help to you. Follow us,' she added, disappearing into the shrubbery, where there was a well-trodden paw-way. Cain and Pierre fell in behind, and when the track met the road, they took the river path leading to a disused local cemetery. Squeezing through a gap in its railings, they made their way to a crumbling mausoleum, half hidden in a dark hollow, surrounded by dense vegetation.

Yvonne said 'this is a special place, linked we think, to Cain's premonition. There's more for you to see, but I'm pregnant, and must have time to give birth before showing you more.'

'But that's terrible,' said Pierre. 'We must get help… we must…'

Yvonne said, 'Calm yourself, *cher* Pierre. We are *cats*. We give birth easily, but I will need a little solitude tonight. It will only mean a slight delay in our plan.'

'If the human men come looking for us,' Cain said to Pierre, 'reassure them that you are well, but must remain by the tomb. And now I sense danger and must return to Molly's garden to protect the kittens in her outhouse. And as long as they are safe, I will return in the morning.'

***

When Molly came home Pierre was nowhere to be seen, and she went straight to the shed, where she counted only ten kittens. She searched the garden again and again but finding nothing, ran to the Penroses'.

'Whatever's the matter?' said Cynthia when Molly burst in through their kitchen door and blurted out that two of her cats were missing. 'Adrian will go mad!' she wailed.

'I didn't know he was mixed up in all this,' said Cynthia.

'My poor little kitties, where are you?' cried Molly, wringing her hands. 'And where's Pierre?'

'Cats can look after themselves,' said Cynthia, 'but Pierre…'

'They'll be together, I'm sure of it,' said Frank, hearing the noise. 'I'll go and get Oliver and we'll look round.'

When he heard the news, his brother said, 'Where would you go if you wanted to *hide* near here?'

'Somewhere quiet,' said Frank, 'along parts of the river path… by the old churchyard. That's it, I'll bet that's where they've gone.'

'Worth a try,' said Oliver, but only when they reached the cemetery did they realise how overgrown and dark it was. They stood for a moment looking through the railings and then, out of the shadows, Pierre materialised and spoke to them.

'What are you doing here?' said Frank, shocked but relieved.

'I'm perfectly well,' said Pierre, 'and Cain's gone back to look after Molly's kittens. Please go home, and I'll see you in the morning.'

Seeing that protesting was useless, the men left, and Pierre curled up in the shrubbery near the tomb and slept soundly.

As soon as it was light, he peered inside the tomb and said, 'How are you, Madame Yvonne?'

A weak voice said, 'Something attacked us in the night. Yvette is dead and I'm dying, and my only live kitten is here. Carry it in your mouth to the human, Molly, and talk to her in her own tongue. Tell her to listen to what it has to say. Go now, go swiftly…'

Pierre pressed his nose against the opening, and she pushed a little bundle towards him, which he grasped in his mouth. He carefully carried it to Molly, who he found in the kitchen, pacing up and down in agitation.

'What have you got there?' she cried.

Pierre gently put down the furry burden he'd been carrying and spoke to her, the first animal ever to do so in spite of her great love for them all.

'Madame Molly,' he said, 'I've come from your missing cats, and I'm sorry but they are dead. One of them, Yvonne, is the mother of this kitten, and was killed to prevent us finding out what it knows. As she lay dying, she said we must listen to what it has to say, and do at once what it tells us to do, however odd that might seem to us.'

4

Molly stared speechless at Pierre, looking up at her with his furry burden wriggling about on the ground between his paws. Then, collecting herself, she said, 'What! *What* did you say?'

'I said we must listen to what this kitten has to say,' he said.

'So, get on with it,' said a tiny, sharp voice, 'I haven't got all day!'

Now it was Pierre's turn to be lost for words, but Molly, recovering faster from her second shock than he was from his first, asked the little creature if it would like some milk.

'An excellent idea, Madame,' squeaked the kitten. 'Slightly chilled and full-fat, please.'

Molly returned with the milk in a saucer, which she placed on the floor. Then, glaring at Pierre, she said, 'I'm going to see Cynthia!'

After she'd gone Pierre regarded his little protégé warily. 'You're very *mature* for a newly born…kitten,' he said, watching it lapping away.

The kitten ignored him until it had finished. 'You

can fill that up,' it said at last, nodding towards the empty saucer.

'I can't, I don't have the paws for it,' said Pierre. 'No opposed thumbs, you know.'

'So, what can you actually *do*?' said the kitten testily.

'I can protect you.'

'Now listen, dog, I can see you're not a bad sort,' said the kitten, 'so take me *very* carefully to somewhere where I can sleep, and wake me *gently* when the humans come back.'

Pierre carried the tiny creature into the sitting room, laid it on the sofa, and stood guard.

***

When Molly found Cynthia, she choked out, 'Pierre's just spoken to me in *English*, and he's brought home a talking kitten. Am I going mad?'

'It takes you like that at first,' said Cynthia. 'My poodle Pommard first spoke to me in English years ago. And then he taught me, Frank and Oliver to speak Canine and Feline. We'll talk about that later, but now we must see to the kitten.'

Pierre, not aware that it was them coming, barked and jumped around a lot, full of sound and fury, signifying not very much.

'Shut up, Pierre,' said Cynthia when they came into the room.

'Good dog,' said Molly, and Pierre wagged his tail, but stopped when he saw it was her.

'Where's the kitten?' said Cynthia, looking around.

'On the sofa,' said Pierre proudly.

'Who are you?' said a sleepy little voice.

'I'm Frank's wife – he found Pierre when he was a puppy,' said Cynthia, 'and I'm so sorry, little one, but your mother has passed on.'

At that, the kitten sat up and said, 'Not quite, for I'm Yvonne's spirit, and you must listen carefully, I haven't much time. Yvette and I were attacked to prevent others finding out that the tomb where I was born is a gateway to other worlds – a *portal*. Tell your neighbours, the Chilvers, what's happened. Speak to them at once, and don't fail me. Or everything will be lost.' The little kitten gasped, the light in its eyes faded and it curled up and died.

The women stared down tearfully at the tiny body, and Pierre gave a low growl.

'And what about the other kittens?' Molly cried, 'Are they in danger?'

'Let's go and see,' said Cynthia, but they saw nothing in the outhouse, and there was no sign of any animal in the garden. 'We'd better speak to the Chilvers,' she said to Molly. 'I'll ask them round tonight. But I really don't know why, they're so dull and ordinary.'

'Why not!' said Molly. 'So far today I've talked with a dog, listened to the spirit of a dead cat in the body of a kitten, and heard about a portal to another world. 'Ordinary' sounds good to me, but somehow I doubt that's how it will turn out.'

***

Doris Chilvers was plump, direct and homely, and her husband, Roland, was grey and heavily bearded, with a warm smile and an attentive manner. They arrived promptly that evening, at Cynthia's invitation, to have a drink. Molly, Frank and Oliver were already there, and formal introductions weren't necessary, for Doris already knew Molly through a mutual friend.

'If it's about Pierre, he doesn't bother us at all,' said Doris, smiling, and breaking the ice.

'That's good to know,' said Cynthia. 'He's partly French, you know.'

Roland smiled, and then turned to Frank, and said, 'When you found him, and he spoke to you, I believe you took it quite calmly.' He smiled and paused. 'I found that most strange. Most people would have turned tail and run away, and tried to forget it ever happened.'

Frank went white and stared at him. 'I don't find it as strange as you knowing he spoke to us!' he gasped.

'Roland, one thing at a time,' said Doris, glaring at her husband. 'Give poor Cynthia a chance to speak.'

She nodded. 'Can we first please go back and talk about why we're here?' she said, and the others listened quietly as she described the events leading up to the kitten's last words.

Doris said, 'You were quite right to take Yvonne's advice and speak to us. But before we get too involved, Molly dear, please take me to where you kept the cats.' She was mystified but agreed when the others encouraged her, and asked Cynthia to come as well. And so all three walked down the road to Molly's house, through the garden to the outhouse, and stood for a moment outside its door.

'Let me go inside alone for a moment,' said Doris, and once inside, she whispered, 'I sense you here,' and slowly, in the darkness, Cain's body became visible.

'It was not a fine cat whose body you used the last time we met, my Lord,' said Doris, 'but in this one you sensed the coming danger, and that has now found its way to me. Is your work here finished now?'

'Not yet,' said Cain's voice, 'but this body was attacked and injured when I came here to guard the kittens, and I will need another one. If I transfer to you now, you can send me into the dog Pierre, before he starts his journey with the human. I de-materialised the kittens to keep them from danger, and I'll restore them now. You can tell the human women that they were hiding, and I was killed protecting them. Now I'll leave this body, so please prepare yourself to receive me. Put my body in the sack you'll find over in the corner, and tell them that you'll bury it to spare them sorrow.'

Molly and Cynthia, although relieved to find the kittens safe, were devastated to hear of Cain's death, but Doris was firm about sparing them further distress, and they trusted her to dispose of his remains. 'This is a sad time,' she said, 'but in spite of our feelings we must not be deflected from the path that lies ahead. And we must now return to discuss with the others how to plan for the future.'

***

'I'm sorry about your cat,' said Roland, when they were together again, 'but we must move on.'

'We're listening,' said Frank.

'First you must accept that we aren't human,' said Doris, 'but we are inhabiting these clumsy little bodies for a reason.'

'So, what are you, and why are you here?' smiled Frank in disbelief.

'We are beings born in the distant past, even before the formation of your galaxy,' said Roland, 'and often remain dormant for many, many of your millennia. But we can be activated if something important needs to be done.'

'So, what has brought you here?' said Oliver.

'We've been assigned to help your species continue to dominate natural life on Earth,' said Roland, 'and also safeguard the portal system.'

'Best to see us as guardians of plant life on planets such as yours,' said Doris.

'Don't think me rude, but why were you chosen?' said Cynthia.

'Frankly,' said Doris, 'it's because, when it came to dealing with Earth and mankind, suddenly no one else was available. And you're a planet with plant life, so here we are.'

'Any *proof* of what you say?' said Frank.

'Ah, party trick time,' said Roland. 'Very well. Close your eyes and concentrate, my friends.'

When they came back from their altered state, the men were white-faced and the women were trembling.

'Now may we proceed?' said Roland, and they all nodded.

'Let's first accept that, through successful biological competition, humanity currently dominates other life-forms on Earth,' said Doris.

'Agreed,' said Oliver.

'When other systems or 'cultures' involving artificial intelligence, often created by natural life-forms, reach a certain complexity,' Roland said, 'a *tipping point* occurs, when the current dominant life-form reacts to the threat to its position.'

'We're nearing that situation on Earth now,' said Frank.

'But what no human knows,' said Doris, 'is that when this point is reached, a Cosmic Constraint operates to select which 'culture' will be the most beneficial for the galaxy. An inquiry is set up to examine the evidence, applicants make their case, a judgement is reached, and action follows.'

'Who makes the judgement?' said Cynthia.

'That's not your concern,' said Roland.

'So why involve us in all this?' said Oliver.

Roland explained that, like it or not, he'd been nominated to be Earth's natural life representative at the Inquiry and, if he was acceptable on the other side of the portal, he would present the case for human dominance.

'I can't take responsibility for the whole human race!' cried Oliver.

'You can, and you will,' said Roland, 'or you wouldn't have been chosen. And when you met Pierre, it was the signal we'd been waiting for.'

'Since we were briefed for this role,' said Doris, 'we've had some time to think about your situation, and feel that the strongest case for human dominance lies not on your dismal record, but on your *potential* to be aware of and tolerant towards other species on the planet. And we think that will best work if you, the chosen human representative, can show that it's possible.'

'Are you mad?' cried Oliver, white-faced with panic.

'We know it's a shock, but when you've finished a journey we've planned for you and Pierre,' said Roland, 'you'll have learned about other life-forms on Earth, and will be able to show how mankind can justify its continuing dominance.'

'No pressure, then,' said Oliver. 'When do we start?'

'Your sense of humour will surely help you along the way,' laughed Roland, 'and you'll need it too. For you'll also have to face another fact of cosmic life – *evil*. It really does exist, and as luck would have it, two entities, both inimical to human life, are very active here at present. The first, called Vormint, has latched onto the foolish publican Adrian because of his occult practices.'

'And there's another much more powerful being, Malesch, resting on Earth at present, that now wants to extend its galactic influence,' said Doris. 'Both of these want to move on, and will want to use the portal system to do that. They will try to 'slipstream' with you when you use it, and we must prevent that, at all costs.'

'It also means you must begin your journey as soon as possible,' said Roland, 'and transit in the portal tonight. I'll see you off and come back after you've gone, and then we must all leave here for a while.'

'What will they find… over there?' asked Molly, who had turned very pale.

'Plenty to do, I imagine,' said Roland. 'Now pack a few things, and we'll meet at seven.'

Molly bit her lip, looked at Oliver and burst into tears. 'Come home with me,' she said.

'Shouldn't we stay together?' said Frank.

'See you two later,' said Cynthia, with a sharp look at Frank, failing as usual to read the signs. And all too quickly, it was last farewells and time for the travellers to leave.

***

To Oliver, the night felt unnaturally still, and the shadows thrown across their path by the light of the full moon seemed so dark that his courage nearly failed him. Roland, jumping when he trod on a dry twig which cracked like a pistol shot, also seemed on edge, and only Pierre appeared unruffled. Then they were off the main path, squeezing through the railings and standing before the monument, its peeling stone façade ghastly white against the black laurels surrounding it. Oliver could hardly bear to look at it, carrying as it did memories of the murder of the cats.

'Is it really a *portal* to other worlds?' he said quietly to Roland, half hoping he would say it was all a fantasy.

'Yes, it really is,' said Roland, sensing his anxiety, and putting an arm around his shoulders. 'It's quite natural for you to be afraid for it's your first time, and everyone always is. Do you trust me when I say that?'

'Yes,' said Oliver quietly.

'Then you must also rely on me telling you there is nothing to fear. A feeling of movement in the comforting dark, which is soon over. Your body will look and feel as it usually does. You will not feel dizzy or sick. And when it is over and the door opens, there will be others to help and guide you on your way.'

'I do hope so,' said Oliver, feeling alone and defenceless.

'It will be so, I promise you. Have faith in them as you have in me. Trust those who have chosen you for this journey and your task. They know what you do not yet know: that your fear of failure is baseless. And they are sure you can, with help, do whatever is asked of you. And that is no small thing.'

At that moment Oliver felt Pierre move towards him, and remembered he also would be facing the unknown. Feeling responsible for another gave him a surge of confidence, and he stroked the great dog's head.

Roland smiled at them both, and in the light of a torch began to look carefully along the wall of the tomb, just above the broken part that acted as their door. He breathed heavily and began feeling over the wall of the tomb, near the great crack that led into the blackness within. After a while he said 'Aha', and began to stroke some marks on the stone, murmuring a simple rhyme.

It was now so still and silent, and he was so keyed-up, that Oliver heard from inside the tomb something like the slightest breath of air. And then a silence so deep that the only sound came from the beating of his heart.

'I've alerted the portal,' said Roland, 'and in a moment it will open. There's no hurry, but it's important that you are both safely inside before I tell it to take you on the first part of your journey.'

'Where are we going?' said Oliver, anxiously.

'Somewhere comfortable, with friends to greet you,' said Roland. 'Good luck.'

Oliver took a deep breath, knelt down and crawled down into the dry, dusty interior of the tomb. Roland pushed Pierre in after him and the big dog scrabbled around before finding his balance. Crushed together like that, Oliver felt a surge of claustrophobia, which passed as Pierre settled down.

'Look at the wall in front of you,' said Roland, 'and you'll see the outline of the portal door.'

Oliver peered into the gloom and, with a beating heart, moved further into the tomb until he approached the wall, dimly illuminated by the faint moonshine entering through the tomb entrance. He touched the uneven surface with his hand, and it was solid, rough and gritty, just an unfinished brick wall. Then he saw a glimmer of red light and slowly, in front of him on the wall, the outline of a door appeared. He hesitated, unsure about what to do.

'Can you see it?' Roland called down from outside.

'Yes, I can see an outline in red light,' he called back.

'Wait until it starts glowing and then just walk into it. It'll feel odd but you've nothing to fear. And don't forget Pierre's coming with you.'

After a moment, the red colour of the outline began to pulse with a golden light and Oliver, watching it, was mesmerised by the unreality of what was happening.

'Go on!' shouted Roland, and, taking a deep breath, Oliver walked into the wall. There was no resistance, and he turned to Pierre, now panting behind him in the dry air, and said, 'Come on, follow me.'

When they had passed through the wall it seemed to Oliver that they were in a space like a dark lift. Then he felt that the aperture behind them was closing and for a second, he felt a whiff of panic. Pierre growled and moved uneasily and Oliver regained his composure when he stroked the dog's head.

And then, as the aperture was on the point of closing, he felt something like a gust of wind sweep past them into the portal. And then the next – and last – thing they heard on their Earth was Roland crying out, 'They got past! My God, I've let them through!' But it was too late, and his words echoed around an empty tomb.

5

Oliver and Pierre stood in what seemed to be a darkened lift, and then felt a slight bump. The door opened and beyond was yet more darkness. Oliver, leading the way, groped blindly around and, holding his arms in front of him, felt something cold and slippery. He instinctively recoiled, lost his balance and grabbed something metallic that yielded, swayed and then lurched towards the ground. He threw himself sideways as the heavy wine rack crashed to the ground, its bottles spewing their contents onto the floor with a mighty shattering of glass. Fine wine cascaded everywhere, and they choked in the heavy fumes as the pungent aroma filled the room.

'My God, now where have we ended up?' gasped Oliver while Pierre growled, shook himself as if emerging from a swim, and began licking the sticky wine from his coat.

And then, high above came the grating noise of an ancient wooden door opening, and looking up they saw a strip of light which widened to show the outlined figure of a man carrying a candelabra. He peered down towards them, and called out in a thin, reedy voice, 'Hallo there, are you alright?' The echoing sound suggested that the cellar was much bigger than Oliver had thought.

'Who's there?' Oliver shouted up.

'I'll come down and help you,' the man said, and slowly descended the stone steps, holding the candelabra in a shaky grip. As he drew near them they could see he was wearing old-fashioned clothes, like an actor in a Victorian play. When he reached them, he smiled at Oliver and then looked about, tutting when he saw the mass of broken glass and the great dark stains spreading out across the floor. He glanced at Oliver, and in spite of his apparent age his eyes were penetrating, bright in the light of the flickering flames.

'This was no accident,' he said. 'Did anything else come through with you?'

'We were about to leave in the portal when our friend shouted that something had got past him,' said Oliver.

'This won't do,' said the man, straightening up, suddenly seeming much younger, 'not here, of all places.' He drew from his waistcoat pocket what looked like a slim silver pen and pointed it around the cellar like a wand. Nothing happened for a moment and then, with a bang, as if a fuse had blown, the pointer was blown from his hand in a cascade of sparks. A second later there was a whoosh and a column of cold air shot up the stairs, surging through the door, which was wrenched back on its rusty hinges.

'The wine distraction didn't work very well for them, did it?' the old man laughed, picking up the candelabra which he'd dropped, and which instantly re-ignited.

'How can you be so relaxed about it?' gasped Oliver.

'Upstairs there are many safeguards against intruders,' said the man. 'Now that we know they are there, I will report what has happened and the necessary action will be taken. I'm Barrett. Please come with me.' He beckoned to them and they followed him up the steep stone steps. Reaching the top, they edged through the ancient wooden door and emerged onto a broad, carpeted corridor.

Barrett led the way along a passage with hunting prints on the walls, from which they entered an elegant Regency-styled reception room, where a tall, slim, silver-haired man was standing, warming his back in front of a blazing fire.

'Welcome to you both,' he said, arms outstretched. He gave a slight bow and said, 'Sebastian, at your service. I understand your arrival was somewhat *dramatic*. Have no fear, those responsible will be apprehended.'

'Where are we, Mr Sebastian?' Oliver asked, wondering how news of their adventure in the wine cellar had reached him already.

'Think of it as the reception of a grand hotel,' said Sebastian. 'I'm assured you had them in your period.'

'Yes, but not many.'

'Then you'll doubtless relish staying here, before you…move on.'

'Where are we going?'

'All in good time,' said Sebastian. 'But first we must prepare to dine. Barrett here will help you dress for dinner, and then we can continue with the evening. Perhaps just you,' he added, looking at Pierre.

'We'll see each other again?' said Oliver, glancing at the dog.

'Tomorrow morning,' said Sebastian, as a footman appeared and asked Pierre to follow him. Meanwhile Barrett conducted Oliver to a dressing room where a selection of formal dress was laid out.

'You'll find any item will fit you perfectly, Sir,' said Barrett. 'Perhaps I might assist you with your choice.' Half an hour later, Oliver, wearing formal evening clothes, including an extravagantly embroidered silk waistcoat, re-joined Sebastian.

'Sir, can you tell me how we got here?' said Oliver, sipping the fine champagne a footman had brought them.

'Ah, not my line at all, *technical* stuff,' Sebastian laughed, 'but here you are, well-dressed, healthy, all safe and sound. That's the main thing. Just the four of us for dinner,' he added. 'Ah, and here are the ladies.' He held out both arms to welcome two beautiful women in evening gowns.

'May I introduce to you Estelle and Lucy,' he said, and Oliver bowed to the ladies, who were wearing low-cut Victorian gowns. They curtsied to him and fluttered their fans.

The four of them then moved into the dining room, where heavy silver cutlery sparkled and cut glass glinted in the light of the candelabras, arranged between elaborate flower arrangements on a polished mahogany table. Eight courses, each with its own wine, was served by an army of footmen, and Oliver found Estelle and Lucy attentive, but elusive if asked about themselves.

'Do you live in this period?' he had asked the one called Estelle.

'Yes and no,' she'd replied.

'We're defined by the epoch to which we're directed,' Lucy had added.

'Think of us without independent existence, forever playing a part,' said Estelle.

'So what role are you playing tonight, here with me?' said Oliver.

'Now, now, ladies,' Sebastian broke in, 'remember you're in *period*, so please confine your conversation to the food, the weather and the season. Whatever that is.'

'Yes, my Lord,' Estelle replied, 'we are prepared for all three.'

And they were as good as their word, but when they parted, both thanked Oliver for his company, and seemed sincere.

***

When he awoke, Oliver inferred from the light that it was morning, although he didn't remember going to bed. There was a soft knock on the door and a manservant appeared with a jug of hot water, which he poured into a basin on the wash-hand stand. He then laid out a cut-throat razor.

'What time is it, please?' asked Oliver.

'Seven o'clock, Sir. Lord Sebastian hopes you will join him for breakfast in the sky-view terrace. I have laid out your own clothes, cleaned and pressed. The lift will take you to his Lordship.'

Oliver shaved carefully, washed and dressed, and, as directed, took the lift outside his room. When the lift stopped, he walked along a corridor and through an open door and entered a spacious, bright room with a white marble floor and a slender vase of blue and white flowers on a sparkling glass table in its centre. Beyond was a dazzling sun-lit terrace where Lord Sebastian was taking breakfast, pouring coffee from a silver pot into a shapely cup. Beside him, Pierre was eating from an alabaster bowl on a low table, while an elegant Borzoi, sleek and beautiful, looked on.

'Good morning,' Pierre said, looking up. 'This is Lady Olga, a dear friend of mine.'

Oliver bowed and the lovely dog said, '*Enchante, monsieur.*'

Sebastian motioned him to a place at the table, a waitress took his order and the others waited while he ate. When he'd finished, his Lordship said, 'Now we must move on – '*festina lente*', as they say – for the journey to prepare you to represent natural life at the Inquiry has already begun. We'll start by acquainting you with two… others, who will be important to you in different ways. Please follow me.'

He led the way down the corridor and opened a door. 'Please stand over there,' he said to Oliver and Pierre, pointing to a circular area in the middle of the room. Then the room darkened and when Oliver looked around, Sebastian had disappeared, and they seemed to be standing on a shimmering path over a dark abyss.

'Ah, so that's a dog,' said a voice. 'Not you, human. Look along the path, and I'll wave.'

Oliver squinted into the dazzling haze, and made out the vague outline of a horse. *Surely not*, he thought, and looked again. The horse waved.

'Who are you?' cried Oliver.

'Worm-like creature,' said the creature, 'how quickly does your Earth move around your sun?'

'Fast enough, I hope,' said Oliver.

'And do you sense any of its movement here?'

'No!' Oliver choked.

'How fast is your sun flying round your galaxy? '

'No idea.'

'And you *still* don't feel a thing, do you, Oliver? But what if you had to keep up with your Earth's orbit under your own steam?'

'Sounds like hard work,' said Oliver.

'Bloody right. Now, how fast is your galaxy moving and where's it going?'

Now Oliver was getting angry, and when Sebastian's voice in his ear gave him the answer, he shouted out, 'We're going towards the Great Attractor at 1.34 million miles an hour and we'll get there in 14 billion years' time.'

'You *cheated* and I'm so angry that I'm going to *do* for you,' roared the animal, rearing up on its front legs. Oliver stood his ground as it charged towards him along the narrow path. *How huge it is,* he thought, fearsome but beautiful too, with its muscular centaur body and torso, and the head of a beautiful cat surmounted by wide-spreading antlers.

'Stop teasing the poor creature, at once!' said a soft voice, and the creature slithered to a halt, towering over

Oliver, where it glared down at him and stamped its hooves.

'Meg,' a familiar voice broke in, 'a fine way to greet our guest!'

'Don't punish him, Lord Sebastian,' pleaded the soft voice, 'he's suffered enough.'

The image faded out, and light returned to the room.

'A thousand apologies,' said Sebastian to Oliver.

'Who was that?' gasped Oliver.

Sebastian said he was Wedros, a chimera: part centaur and satyr, with a dash of faun. His father was Wrach, an aggressive centaur, and his mother Meg a were-cat, a powerful shapeshifter, big-hearted and beautiful. Wedros had just 'done time' in Earth's orbit for misconduct, and this had doubtless led to his bad behaviour.

'I do apologise, I'd quite forgotten that he's such a *giddy* creature, all whirling whim and base emotion,' said Sebastian, 'and quite off-script! He was supposed to *help* you acclimatise! But he's merely foolish, not dangerous like the entity on whom you'll now be eavesdropping. Meet Controller Ovoid. Stay in the circle only, Oliver, please,' he added. 'Pierre will join you later.'

The room darkened, and Oliver was now looking down on a cramped little office containing a plywood desk, behind which sat a small, fat, red-faced man in a brown suit, talking to another man standing in front of him, nervously twisting a trilby hat.

'Controller Ovoid,' the man said, 'we've got an application from the Centre of an average-sized spiral galaxy, which locals call the 'Milky Way.''

'What do they want?'

'Their place in the sun, or rather their sun in a place on the Council of a Hundred Thousand Suns. Responsible, as you know, for the governance of the galaxy's hundred billion suns. The star's four billion years old, an average suburban yellow dwarf, with a life expectancy of five billion Earth years. Rocky planets near the centre, giant gaseous and icy ones further out.'

'How unusual. Guarantees?'

The man said, nervously, that the applicants would put up one of the small rocky planets against any malfeasance in office. One the locals called 'Earth,' at present dominated by an organic species.

'"Organic," you say?' said the Controller, squinting pointedly.

'If forfeited it would, of course, be thoroughly sanitised.'

'And who's going to pay for that? Application refused.'

The man stammered that the sun was located in the *Grade One Listed Cold Light Matter* sector of the galaxy.

'Rare, but not remarkable.'

'But as warm dark matter and energy make up at least 99.9% of universal…'

'Ah, at last, a lesson in basic celestial mechanics,' said the Controller. 'Please say 'yes' if you think I need one.'

'Yes, Sir. I mean no, Sir. You don't. Need it, I mean,' stammered the man. 'But *if* the local Centre's application was successful, and it breached some trivial regulation, thereby forfeiting the 'Earth,' such a planet might be attractive in some quarters as an addition to its Rare Planet Collection. The donor of a similar planet recently gifted in this way received an extra dimension, and its Controller was richly rewarded.'

'Promising candidate,' said the Controller. 'Let them submit more details.'

The vision faded and light returned to the room.

'Is Ovoid for real?' said Oliver.

'Possibly,' said Sebastian, cheerfully. 'Real enough to be powerful.'

'He seems to hate organic life.'

'Of course. He's an *Artificial,* and entities like him can be touchy about Naturals,' said Sebastian. 'Perhaps he just likes things orderly and neat. Natural life's not always *tidy,* is it? All dangly bits and unsavoury habits, not to mention the smell.'

'But none of this is *real,* is it?' said Oliver. 'Creatures like satyrs and centaurs really are *mythical,* aren't they?'

'Ah, that word 'real',' Sebastian smiled. 'I could cite a dozen worlds where humans would be considered most unlikely.'

'Does a *true* reality exist?' said Oliver, despairingly. 'One accepted by all creation?'

'When I'm asked that – and I always am – I have to say that *my* true reality is likely to be unreal to them. And vice versa. Then I usually just talk about the weather, or sex with fifty... legs or something.'

'Is there a real *you,* Lord Sebastian?'

'There's a form I liked to use more than others.'

'What did it look like?'

'I suppose to you it would appear as a complex algorithm written in light on a wind-blown, moving cloud, changing like smoke as it got solved. Don't know by whom, of course.'

'What did the Controller look like to you?' said Oliver.

Sebastian looked puzzled. 'His usual pinkish-grey misty form,' he said, 'with a reddish light in its centre, pulsating as it always does when he gets upset. And nearby was a smaller, dimmer light.'

'That must have been the man twisting his hat in his hands,' said Oliver.

'There you are, you see,' said Sebastian, 'I could never have imagined anything as strange as that! Now you need to say goodbye to Pierre, who knows you must journey alone for the present. Just one other thing, though.'

'Yes?' said Oliver, with a sinking feeling.

'Don't forget you transited yesterday,' said Sebastian, 'and the world we're on now is your Earth's Shadow-side. You'll find it's *slightly* different from your birth planet.'

'It doesn't feel very 'shadowy,' said Oliver.

'No, it won't, but it *is* different.'

'In what way?'

'You'll have to find that out for yourself, I'm afraid,' said Sebastian, 'because *your* version of your own world is personal and unique to you. And even though you'd share much of what's different here with others from your birth world, it wouldn't necessarily be the *same* difference.'

'I'll have to think about that,' said Oliver.

'Best to think of it as a mirror image of your world, with some extra bits.'

'Like what?'

'You must learn to *accept* there are things that you cannot know,' said Sebastian, 'so don't try to understand everything that comes your way. A proper sense of awe is the mark of a mature being.'

'I'll try,' said Oliver.

'Good. Now close your eyes, and think hard about somewhere nice, where you were happy. Some childhood memories are good for that.'

Oliver concentrated and then he was falling, down and down. And of the hotel where he'd stayed there was nothing left but his memory, no reception or sky terrace, dining room or wine cellar, not anything, just *nothing*. But he carried his own inner world with him as he fell, with all its thoughts and feelings, and even a few of its dreams.

6

Oliver landed with a bump on springy grass, rolled over and sat up. Looking around, he knew at once where he was: in a meadow high in the English southern Cotswolds. He'd known it since he was a boy and, when it was clear, from here he could glimpse the mysterious Forest of Dean, far away beyond the shining River Severn winding its way to the Bristol Channel.

Lying there, he reflected on what had happened since transiting in the portal with Pierre. Being here, with dewdrops sparkling on the leaves of grass, everything seemed as natural as he remembered it long ago. Then he felt a movement in the grass and, looking down, saw a large insect, its opalescent body radiating fierce energy, gossamer wings glittering in the sunlight. In a flash it was gone, and Oliver was stunned, certain that he'd never seen anything like that before anywhere on Earth. And yet here it was, alien to him, but also totally at home!

He remembered Sebastian's words about Earth's Shadow-side being subtly different and wondered what other surprises lay ahead. Then his eye caught a movement by the hedge bordering the field in which he lay and, shading his eyes, he saw in the nearby lane a woman waving to him from behind a gate. Jumping to his feet, he ran across the field to meet her.

'Welcome, Oliver,' she said, shaking his hand. 'I'm Meg, your guide for the next part of your journey.'

'Hello Meg,' he said. 'Where have I heard your name recently?'

'Perhaps you overheard me speaking to Lord Sebastian,' she said.

'That's it,' said Oliver, 'about your son, Wedros.'

'He didn't frighten you too much, I hope.'

'I was scared out of my wits,' said Oliver.

'He suffered cruelly when he was young,' she said, 'a little feline centaur, so different from the rest. Children can be terribly unkind, especially the under-five hundreds. No wonder, he got into bad company, and he was savagely punished by having to circle your Earth for thousands of years, keeping you safe from asteroids, not to mention clearing up your disgusting space debris.'

Oliver, still feeling that Wedros was a bully and a lout who could benefit from many more terrestrial circuits, thought it best not to reply.

'He's not that bad,' said Meg abruptly, turning towards the road. 'Come on, I'll explain more when we're on our way.'

She led him to where a camper van was parked near woodland by the side of the lane, and when they reached it she opened the door and sat in the driver's seat. Oliver climbed into the passenger seat and she smiled across at him. *How beautiful she is,* he thought, looking at the thick, luscious hair framing the pale face with its enormous green eyes, like those of a lovely cat.

But as he watched her smile faded, and she seemed alarmed. 'Something's coming,' she said, looking anxiously around, 'and it's not good, whatever it is.' Looking back to where they had come from, Oliver saw a dense black fog sweeping down over the slope of the field where he'd arrived, a shadow racing across the ground, like moving clouds blotting out the sun on a windy day. He felt a sudden chill as the darkness surged towards them, and gasped for air as heavy wreaths of mist rose up from the ground. And, as he watched, a whirlwind of black air quivered and whirled in the centre of the cloud – an unstable column, streaked with dark red stripes, yellow vapour pouring from its periphery like pus from a wound.

'Get out, now!' screamed Meg. 'Into the woods as fast as you can, and keep going. Don't stop and don't look round. I'll handle what's coming, it's far beyond you.'

He opened his door and she pushed him out violently, her cuff creeping back to expose silky fur beginning to cover her exposed wrist. Oliver hit the ground and, looking back for an instant, saw her leap out of the van and begin running towards the storm, growing catlike at a frightening rate. Her hands were sprouting into huge claws, her great, green eyes were gleaming, the prominent breasts were sinking into her chest, and whiskers were appearing above teeth drawn into a feral scowl. Raw power was pouring from her as she stopped and turned to face the oncoming onslaught.

Oliver, running for dear life, stumbled at first and then plunged into the trees. He crashed on and on through the undergrowth, scrambled through a wire fence, blundered into a mass of laurel and rhododendron bushes and, gasping for breath, stumbled upon the sunlit putting green of a golf course.

When he'd recovered, he looked around and listened. Hearing nothing, he crept back to the edge of the green, parted the dense shrubs and peered back into the wood. It was empty and silent, except for the faint touch of a morning breeze, and the gentle rustle of dead leaves as some small animal foraged beneath the trees.

He began retracing his steps and then stopped to think. Dare he return to the camper van? He quailed at the thought of what might have happened there, but decided he had no choice. He started walking slowly, trying to pick up traces of his headlong flight, but soon realised that he'd run much further than he'd thought. He looked around and knew that he was lost. Beginning to feel the stress of his flight, his knees weakened and he leant against a tree, faint and disorientated. He fought down the panic he was feeling and then, pulling himself together, he ran on. But blundering through some bushes he felt the ground give way, and fell heavily into a sunken lane.

'You're on an ancient way, you know,' said a voice, 'old, long before the Romans came.'

'Who's there?' Oliver cried out, but there was no answer.

'You're early. Where's Meg?' said the voice, and Oliver looked around, intrigued rather than frightened, for the voice, with its reedy quality, possessed a kind of natural reassurance and held no threat,

'I left her by the camper van near the lane by the field,' he said. 'A terrible whirlwind appeared, and she began morphing to face it. She told me to escape into these woods, and I ran until I reached a golf course, and now I'm trying to return to her camper van.'

'It's lucky for you she was there to help,' said the voice. 'A whirlwind, you say. *Notice* anything about it, did you?'

'Like what?'

'Any noise? Or a smell, like burning rubber? Or sulphur.'

'Are you serious? No, none of those things. Do you know what it was?'

'No. Is there anything you want? Food, drink?'

'I'm very hungry,' said Oliver.

'It's rather short notice,' said the voice, 'but I could lay my roots on some nice, plump earthworms, a cold collation of slugs and snails (*escargots*, should I say) or some caterpillars, which I have been keeping, possibly a *little* past their best. Or perhaps you'd prefer something veggie, like reeds or tree-bark. Or do soil-fresh truffles sound more appealing?'

'Actually, I'm not all *that* hungry,' said Oliver, quickly, 'and I really *must* get back to the van.'

'Very well, but you'll need a guide,' said the voice, and shouted, 'Magpie! Magpie! Stop doing that! Oliver's early and needs to connect with Lady Meg. He'll help you find her campervan.'

In a moment a pert black and white bird appeared

from within a nearby bush, into which it squirted a white stream from its rear. Ignoring the cry of rage that issued from the foliage, it flew off into a nearby tree, landed on a branch and looked back at Oliver.

'Come on, then,' it said to him, 'I haven't got all day.'

'Sorry,' said Oliver, pulling himself up short when he realised he was apologising to a wild bird. 'Go on, I'm following you.'

'You'd better,' said the bird and flew off from tree to tree, in the process winging aside several smaller birds occupying their chosen branches. It looked back from time to time to make sure Oliver was following, and soon they reached the camper van. There was no-one around and Oliver peered into the passenger window.

'Don't worry, pussy's gone,' said an irritated voice, and Oliver looked around to see who'd spoken.

'It's still me, the magpie, up here!' said the bird, which then hopped down onto the roof of the van.

'Who were you speaking to before we met?' Oliver asked.

'Brian, the shrub spirit,' said the bird.

'Do you mean a tree spirit, like a Dryad?' said Oliver.

'An inferior sub-species in his case,' said the bird, 'can't pass the exams for the big stuff, can't Brian. You need a Higher Natural to look after growths higher than a satyr's horns, and he's no good at exams.'

'Is he… rooted to the spot, as it were?' asked Oliver.

'Has to put in a certain amount of time planted, the rest of the time he's free to do what he wants.'

'What does a tree-shrub want to do?'

All the magpie knew was that Brian usually assumed a human form when he was off-duty, travelled around a lot, and was big on the National Trust. 'By the way, this is his campervan you've *purloined*,' he said, 'and he won't like that one little bit. Nor will his friends. Can turn very nasty, those hedgerow types.'

'I thought it belonged to Meg,' said Oliver anxiously.

'No. And sadly, I might feel honour-bound to speak up about the theft,' said the magpie.

'Must you?' said Oliver.

'I'll be honest with you,' said the bird, 'I'm supposed to help you on your journey, but it's difficult if I'm only a magpie. Now if I was a *hawk...*'

'How would that help?'

The bird ignored the question and from its vantage point on the van, bent its head down low and whispered to Oliver. 'I'm a trans-avian, and if you help me reincarnate, I'll come back as a kestrel. Called 'Kes.' Think of that.'

'What would I have to do?'

'Kill me, of course.'

'That's murder!'

'Well, I can't resurrect if I'm still alive, can I?' said the magpie.

'How would I do it?' gasped Oliver.

'Cut my throat, bash me on the beak with a brick, strangle me. Apart from poison, which is too slow, I don't care.'

'I just *couldn't*,' stammered Oliver.

'Look, Mr Squeamish, why not run me over?' said the bird. 'I'll even tell you the words to say while you're doing it.'

Oliver, now beyond caring, noticed that Meg had left the keys in the ignition and reluctantly agreed. The magpie fluttered down to the front of the vehicle and composed himself on the ground in front of the nearside front wheel. He arranged his wings in a dignified fashion, relaxed, closed his eyes and told Oliver the words he had to say as he ran him over. Then he said, 'Go ahead,' and with his heart beating wildly, Oliver climbed into the driver's seat, started the engine, put it in gear and drove it forward. There was a slight bump. He stopped the van and walked back to inspect the magpie, who looked very peaceful, rather flatter and quite dead. Oliver felt a lump in his throat. His reverie was interrupted by an angry screech from above.

'I can't hover up here all day, waiting for you. Let's get this over with.'

Oliver looked up and saw a kestrel fluttering above him, 'You've reincarnated!' he cried.

'Of course not, you fool, he's not some damned phoenix!' cried the kestrel. 'My wife will be along any moment with the egg.'

'What egg?' said Oliver.

'I suppose you do know that birds start off as eggs,' said the kestrel, 'and she's coming now, so get something to put it in.'

'Like what?'

'A shoebox. There's probably one in the back of the van.'

Oliver opened the door and, to his surprise, found a box with some cotton wool inside it. He placed it open on the roof, and a smaller kestrel fluttered down with an egg in its claws, gently deposited it in the box, and then flew off with her husband. Oliver placed the box on the passenger seat and wondered what to do. His musings were cut short by a cracking noise coming from inside the shoebox, which he gently opened. Peeping inside, he saw the egg lying in pieces, and beside it a tiny brown fledgling.

'I'm starving,' it said, looking up at him.

Oliver guessed that the best chance of getting Kes the right food would be from a pet shop, and the nearest one would be in Gloucester. He backed the van onto the lane, and then took the main road running through pretty beech woods as it descended steeply from the Cotswold plateau. The road twisted and turned, and the shoebox on the passenger seat shifted from side to side.

'What about my food?' said the fledgling. 'Any roadkill on you?'

'Of course not,' said Oliver. 'We'll get you something in a pet shop in Gloucester.'

'Just remember,' said Kes, 'I'm not some pet, but a wild, free-flying hawk. Or will be,' he added darkly, 'if I ever get some food to keep beak and feathers together.'

They bumped and shuddered their way into Gloucester with its lovely cathedral, litter-filled streets, empty shops and dirty municipal buildings. Oliver spotted a dingy pet shop in a grubby Victorian side street, parked the van and, carrying the shoebox under his arm, pushed open the door of the shop, which opened with an old-fashion 'ting'.

Inside it smelt of bird droppings, stale tortoise salad, stagnant green water and bone meal. There were unlikely combinations for sale like goldfish and fishing tackle, hamsters and mousetraps. A thinly bearded man in a brown overall with filthy hands and bitten nails was introducing flies to a container housing hungry lizards, and was having difficulty in overcoming the reluctance of the insects to fully embrace their role.

He looked up as Oliver entered the shop, his thin smile dying stillborn when he saw that he was carrying a shoebox. Like brown envelopes arriving in the post for others, good things seldom came to pet shop owners when people arrived with such articles under their arms.

'What can I do for you, mate?' he said with a strong West Country burr, accentuated by a severe shortage of teeth.

'I need to give my bird some food,' said Oliver, opening the box on the counter. 'What would you suggest?'

They both looked inside, and he was astonished to see how big Kes had grown, with creamy-white down on his body, and disproportionately large feet.

'Wild bird, you've got there, squire,' said the shop-keeper, 'there's a law about capturing them, specially ones like him. Lethal for my prize racing pigeons, his kind. I'd kill them all if I had my way.'

Kes shifted restlessly and seemed to look enquiringly at Oliver.

'Found him as a fledgling,' he explained, 'my kids love him. Promised them I'd look after him.'

'You know what you've got there, don't you?'

'A little kestrel. My kids call him 'Kes'.'

'My friend,' said the man, 'look at the size of his feet.'

Oliver became acutely aware that a small pair of glittering eyes were fixed on him with a ferocious glare.

'He's a peregrine falcon, most like, and a male I should think.' He picked Kes up and inspected his body in an intimate way. 'Yes, you've got a tiercel there, mate, smaller than the female, but just as deadly to my racing pigeons, the little sod.' He shook the bird for a moment, and then placed him back in the shoebox.

'One of the fastest birds in the world!' said Oliver.

'Yep, when he goes into a stoop,' said the man, 'and then bang into one of my prize pigeons, which is dead on arrival, when it reaches the ground.'

'I'll do for this creep's pigeons when I grow up, every one of them, see if I don't,' said Kes through a gritted beak. 'Abused by a bloody chick molester, and me, a noble peregrine falcon.'

Oliver looked anxiously at the owner to see if there was any reaction to Kes talking, but as he seemed unaware of anything out of the ordinary, he said, 'What does he eat?'

'Bloody racing pigeons.'

'Anything else?'

'Yes, other birds. Get him a chicken sandwich.'

'Are you going to take much more of this?' screeched Kes. 'Punch him out.'

'I'll do no such thing,' said Oliver, and then looked at the man, who was regarding him in a puzzled way. 'Seriously, what do you recommend?' he said.

The man shrugged and suggested warm fresh protein which was easily portable. He recommended a 'bumper boxful' of wriggling worm bait, some best Euro-worms, a few African Night Crawlers and some Jersey Jumpers.

'You'd like that wouldn't you, nasty little fowl?' he said, poking Kes with a grimy finger.

'Do I look like a sodding fish?' screamed Kes, biting the finger as hard as he could. The atmosphere was becoming painfully frigid, so Oliver paid promptly, and he left with a plentiful supply of red mealworms and the shoebox under his arm.

'Maybe you'll show a bit more respect now you know you've got a peregrine tiercel in the family,' said the voice from the shoebox when they got back to the van. 'And I'll soon have no room in here – we grow very quickly, we incarnates.'

'What do we do now?' said Oliver. 'I'm worried about Meg. I hope she's alright. Will she contact us, do you think, Kes?'

'Lance.'

'What?'

'My name – short for 'Lancelot'. I'm not just a common kestrel, am I?'

'Whatever you say,' said Oliver, wearily. 'But what do we do now?'

The bird put its head to one side and seemed to be hearing something. 'Alright, alright, I can hear you,' he said. 'Ten o'clock, tomorrow, by the big oak. Don't worry, I'll be quite comfortable sleeping in my shoebox, for now, and we've got plenty of food'.

'Who were you speaking to?' said Oliver.

'That was Brian,' said Lance. 'He wants us to sleep in the van tonight, and then we're to drive to meet him at ten o'clock in the morning. I know where.'

'And I suppose we can both sleep in the shoebox, can we?' said Oliver. 'And share out the Jersey Jumpers for supper.'

'As long as you leave some for me,' said Lance.

7

After an uncomfortable night in the van Oliver woke early, and Lance told him where they could meet Brian. They drove to a pleasant little park overlooking a small river, and on the seat beneath a large oak tree sat a tall, youngish man, with a pleasant tanned face, reading a copy of 'The Field'. He was wearing a well-cut Prince of Wales check suit, expensive brogues and a dark felt trilby, making him look like a prosperous racehorse owner at a fashionable meeting. Oliver got out of the van and approached him. Seeing him coming, the man held out his hand and smiled.

'Hello, I'm Brian,' he said. 'I sent the magpie to help you after that business with Meg.'

'He's in the shoebox in the van,' said Oliver.

'Leave him there for a moment,' said Brian, quietly, 'while we have a little word here.' They sat together under the oak.

'Did the bird refer to me?' he said.

Oliver hesitated and then said, 'He told me you were a shrub-spirit who couldn't pass woodland exams.'

That seemed to please Brian, who nodded and said, 'Good. In all modesty I'm rather more than that, for I've been in deep cover for many ages, helping to protect this planet's woodland realm. That's why I've been asked to help you become more familiar with natural life on your own world, and here on the Shadow-side.'

'Do you know what happened to Meg after I got away?' said Oliver.

'I sent a kestrel to find out what happened,' said Brian, 'and she saw a huge brown patch on the field, where the grass had been badly damaged.'

'Any sign of Meg?' said Oliver.

'No,' said Brian, 'but I'd have heard if she'd been injured. And as for the grass, I just couldn't leave it like that. So I got a nest of leaf-cutting ants to clear it up, and later that night I re-seeded the whole area.'

'What was that *hurricane*?' said Oliver. 'I've never seen anything like it.'

'Oliver,' said Brian, 'first, understand that something is out to destroy the case for human dominance on Earth, and anything that will promote it is in danger. They will stop at nothing to harm you on your journey.'

'By doing what?' said Oliver, dreading the answer.

'Deep breath, Oliver,' said Brian. 'By killing you.'

'I suppose I knew that,' said Oliver, miserably, 'but what *was* it in that field?'

'It was something we call a 'fear-tracer,' said Brian. 'Its purpose was to create a very frightening experience for you, so that it could capture your reactions and use these permanent 'fear vibrations' to track your future movements.'

'Do you think I'm affected?' said Oliver.

'Not as far as we can tell,' said Brian, 'or we'd have known by now.'

'What did Meg do?'

'She diverted it, and without you there, it dissipated.'

'What caused it?' said Oliver.

'Perhaps something that got through with you when you first transited.' said Brian.

'You heard about that?'

'Yes. Sebastian's people looked into the intruder in your 'hotel' wine cellar, and found that Malesch, a powerful, evil creature, as well as Vormint, crossed with you in the portal. They *might* be connected with the attack, or not. We don't yet know.'

Oliver said nothing. He was amazed that all these apparently disconnected beings seemed to know what each other were doing. He found the idea rather comforting.

'Let's return to the van, and see to the magpie,' said Brian. 'He must be cramped in that box.'

'I helped him re-incarnate,' said Oliver. 'He's not a magpie anymore.'

'He's only just *become* one!'

'If I didn't help him reincarnate, he said he'd tell you I stole your van,' said Oliver.

'What is he now?' Brian sighed.

'A peregrine falcon.'

'That bird!' said Brian. 'When he first came to the woodland realm he was a feral city pigeon called Phil, who set up as a nest agent and ran a protection racket with an enforcer, Errol the cuckoo. A lot of birds lost nests when they'd finished with them, but *they* made a fortune. And then came the social climbing. Phil met a lovely bird, blown off course, from Africa, and the word was that she knew about reincarnation. He was now living it up in what he called his 'big drum' of a nest, and took her under his wing, and that was the last anyone saw of her.'

'Next thing, he's gone, the nest's sold for a fortune, and along comes an owl called Henry, with an East-End accent, who gets a weaver-bird to build him a designer residence called 'Mon Eyrie' in an up-market oak, for which he paid with a wad of worms two inches thick.'

There was an uneasy stirring from inside the shoebox.

'The Woodland Court got wind of his doings,' said Brian, 'and only two lunars ago he was sentenced to assist me for a hundred years. Then he appeals, playing the 'trans' card, because as an owl he said he could only work nights. The idiots agreed, and that's why, when you met him, he was a magpie.'

'He calls himself 'Lancelot', said Oliver.

'Phil, Henry, Lancelot – who cares?' said Brian. 'He still has to work for me, and now I've got a peregrine falcon with temperament, instead of a magpie with attitude. Now we really must move on, but I'll change first, and then speak to him.'

He disappeared into the back of the van, and Oliver opened the lid of the shoebox, took out the fledgling and placed in front of it an open tin of wriggling red mealworms.

'Ugh,' said Lance, but nevertheless set to with a will.

'By the way,' Oliver said, 'Brian wants a word.'

'Oh,' said the falcon, uneasily, 'what about?'

'Who knows?' said Oliver.

When Brian emerged from the van he was bearded and wearing a scruffy anorak and a woollen hat. 'Got to get into character with the van,' he said. 'And now I'll have a little chat with… Lance, here. Please excuse us.' He picked up the bird, placed it in the shoebox and carried it out of earshot. When he came back, he said, 'That's all settled then. Lance knows that I expect him to warn, protect and obey you. Now let's go, no time to lose.'

'Where are we going?' said Oliver.

'To Coleford, in the Forest of Dean,' said Brian. 'More precisely, to the Speech House, to meet your next guide. I don't know who it will be, because we're running a bit ahead of the planned schedule, and I don't know why you're going there, either. 'Need to know', standard procedure.'

To get to the forest they needed to return to Gloucester, cross the Severn and drive west along the road towards south Wales. At first the traffic was heavy and Brian drove in silence, but as the road became quieter, he spoke to Oliver.

'You must be getting confused,' he said.

'Not at all,' Oliver replied. 'It's quite normal for me to travel with a shrub spirit and a reincarnated peregrine falcon, following an encounter with a delinquent feline-cross centaur and a huge morph-cat, after an evening dining in a spectral grand hotel and watching the Controller of the Galaxy at work.'

'Don't lose that sense of humour,' smiled Brian, 'it'll keep you sane.'

'Where exactly did you say we were going?' said Oliver.

'Somewhere called the Speech House,' said Brian, 'where, as I said, you'll meet your next guide. I bet she knows Meg – they like to use people who know each other on important journeys. And Meg likes you, I understand.'

'That's good to hear,' said Oliver. 'Best chums with a huge were-cat, who spends time in different dimensions, no doubt chasing gigantic mice.'

'I don't suppose she often does that,' laughed Brian. 'It must be your sense of humour that appeals to her. Not much to amuse a being in the cold reaches between the stars, where she seems to spend most of her time.'

That took some digesting and Oliver was silent for a while. 'What about you?' he said. 'What happens when you're not *rooted*?'

Brian looked down at the box containing Lance, winked at Oliver, and said that 'shrub-folk' like him had a time-share arrangement, but it was first-come first-served, as everyone wanted a tropical island in which to warm their roots, rather than being frozen in permafrost in a remote tundra.

After another hour a line of trees appeared, marking the start of the forest, and the early morning sun, glinting between patches of rising mist, had disappeared. Low, dark clouds, heavy with moisture, were gathering as they turned off the main road along a narrow road, and then took a dirt track, taking them deep into the brooding woods.

'There's somewhere ahead where you can spend the night,' said Brian, 'and then we'll drive on to your meeting at the Speech House in the morning.'

The van bumped and creaked its way along the track, stopping beside a hut in a gloomy clearing, where an old stone bridge spanned a small, fast-flowing stream. Brian stopped the car, seemed to listen to something, and said, 'Sorry, but I must leave you until the morning. Don't worry, if things get tricky the forest will protect you, and I've accelerated Lance's growth. From now on you'll always be able to trust him.'

Oliver picked up the shoebox and got out of the van, which spun around and roared off with Brian waving an arm from the open window. Silence returned to the clearing and he looked around, feeling vulnerable and alone. Then the peace was shattered by an imperious voice coming from the shoebox. 'Get me out,' shouted Lance. 'I want to practise flying.'

'You're too young to fly,' said Oliver.

'I assume these wing things I've got sticking out on either side will help if they're allowed to,' came the irritated reply.

Oliver slowly opened the box, and crammed inside, was a large, immature hawk. 'You're beautiful,' he breathed, gently lifting it out.

'Just wait until you see me in action,' said Lance. 'Hold out your arm for me to perch on.' With a flutter of wings, he balanced himself, turned the yellow eyes in his cruel-beaked head to look at Oliver, and said, 'Well, go on then, give me a flying start!'

Oliver threw his arm into the air. There was a thrashing of feathers and a beating of wings and Lance was up and away. Unsteadily at first, but then with amazing rapidity, he wheeled away and tore upwards, until he was just a dot high in the sky. And then he was gone, and Oliver was left standing alone in the middle of the wood.

He looked inside the hut and saw a wooden table, on which was a package of sandwiches and some fruit. He took the food with some he'd saved for Lance from the van, and sat on a rough bench by the side of the stream, aware now that the sky was getting darker and a chill wind was springing up. He was hungry but his anxiety took away his appetite and he left the sandwiches, preferring to watch the water in the stream curling and twisting through the low, moss-covered stone bridge. He wondered why he felt so uneasy among the dense woods beneath the scudding clouds.

Suddenly there was a flurry of wings and a large hawk landed on a nearby branch. 'That felt good,' said Lance, and Oliver stared at his beautiful strong body with its broad shoulders, white breast speckled with dark single feathers, and closely barred white undersides.

'My goodness, Lance, you grew quickly,' said Oliver.

'It was decided you'd need protection and, *voila*, here I am,' said the hawk. 'And I've got some special powers too – only temporary ones, of course.'

'Powers?'

'To help me *investigate* what might be coming,' said Lance. 'And talking of that, something's in the wind, and I must find out more. But first I'll teach you how to call me, and when you do, I'll always come as quickly as I can.'

After he had taught Oliver the 'summons' he flew away, leaving him to walk back to the hut. Inside it felt comfortable and warm, and, after lighting the candle on the table, he flopped onto the bed and fell fast asleep. He awoke feeling refreshed in spite of vivid dreams, sat up and looked at his watch. He couldn't believe he'd been asleep for so long, and when he looked out of the window, he saw that it was beginning to get dark. Judging from the soaking foliage, it had rained whilst he slept, and by the look of the heavy, dirty-white clouds in the dark sky, there was more to come.

He began to feel a terrible anguish, all the worst for being inexplicable, and some instinct warned him not to stay in the hut. He stepped outside into the darkening evening, walking slowly towards the trees, damp and dripping after the rain, his heart pounding. His fear made him deeply sensitive to what was around him, and it came to him that beneath the roots of the trees lay dark mysteries of things best left to themselves.

Meanwhile above ground, he sensed the myriad smells brought out by the recent rain and, underpinning the natural odours, another that was acrid, unfamiliar and unpleasant. Now on the alert he looked around, noticing that the earth around the hut had been disturbed as he slept, and his stomach lurched.

He crossed the bridge over the stream, pausing to look down at the swirling water. A city dweller for most of his life, he felt how *alien* it was here, and lonely too, for he had no friends with him or anything to give him a feeling of being at home. The silence of the setting felt oppressive and menacing, and even the drips from the trees began to torment him.

And then his blood froze, for beyond the stream near the hut he thought he saw the ground begin to move. He stared and what he had imagined was all too true. It was as if great earthworms burrowing near the surface were pushing up giant furrows, and between the heaving folds, their skin oozing a thick yellow pus, huge creatures with bloated worm-like bodies supported by black, hairy, spiny legs were slithering across the fractured ground towards the hut, creating a black, writhing mat. And as Oliver watched, mesmerised and nauseated, the moving matter paused and, as if sensing something, changed direction and began sliding towards the bridge where Oliver was standing. As it neared the stream, the mass of creatures seemed to become obscenely excited, the parts coalescing and thickening and rising up into the semblance of a huge stumbling human figure, searching urgently to right and left, as if tasting the air.

'Help! Somebody help me!' Oliver screamed in an agony of fear, in the nick of time remembering to utter the cry that Lance had taught him. Almost at once, with a flash of feathers and a rush of air, the heavy hawk fell from the sky onto his outstretched arm. 'Oh, help me, Lance,' said Oliver faintly, 'help me.'

'Follow the rabbit,' said the bird, and flew away.

Oliver looked around and saw the animal's white tail just visible in the deepening gloom. He ran after it into the wood for all he was worth, and plunged into the undergrowth as the rabbit disappeared into a burrow beneath the threshing trees. An unseen branch seemed to push him sideways and he fell into a deep hollow in the ground, where smaller branches instantly wove themselves together, covering him and pinning him down. He struggled in their grasp as more foliage formed a dark roof over his body, followed by moss and forest litter cascading down to fill the gaps.

It was useless to try to move, and he just lay there hardly able to breathe. The wind, which seemed to have arisen as the awful shape appeared, died away, branches fell limp, leaves drooped and the only sound was the sullen drip of rainwater. Gradually Oliver became aware of subtle noises around him: scrapings and scrabblings, whisperings and hissings. And, although he'd grown up in sterile, artificial surroundings, he thought he *recognised* these sounds, and *felt* rather than simply heard them. For here were the sounds of the living forest, its flora and fauna, its insects and its wood-wide web of filaments and tendrils. All the progeny of wind-borne seeds, pods and berries, germinating and passing on the life-force, a complex natural web, so unknown to most modern humans.

Then the terror returned. First the earth trembled, the noise swelled and the air grew heavy and oppressive. Oliver's eyes lost focus, his eardrums felt as if they were imploding, and his nostrils recoiled from a rank odour. The ground shook violently like a wet dog leaving water, a deep booming bore down on the earth and the trees began tossing wildly again.

And then, out of this fog of confusion, came the entity, now more elephantine and lumbering than ever, blundering on, like a blind creature seeking prey. Oliver, now far beyond terror, had reached a calm acceptance of his death, coupled with a profound sadness and a piercing compassion for the creature, which paused, as if sensing his feelings.

Suddenly a shocking pain struck him in the side, so acute it seemed alive, and he gasped and writhed to ease the grip of a branch that had swung against him, pressing hard into his side. After a moment it relaxed and pulled away, and as it did so he realised that the beast had moved on. Only then did he realise that the pain, suffusing his whole mind, had deflected the monster's gaze at a critical instant.

And then, at last, he saw it all and he saw it whole. The Earth, through the woods, had offered him succour in his hour of need. And now, as the heaviness in the air lifted, branches loosened around him and the moss fell away from his face. He staggered to his feet, went a few steps and then turned, faced the trees and bowed to the wood with his hand on his heart. He said, 'Thank you for saving me, as one day I hope to save you.' A breath-like breeze shimmered through the bushes and trees, like a murmur of accord, and Oliver felt a deep oneness with all the living things around him, and for an instant a well of happiness as strong as any emotion he'd ever felt swelled up inside him.

'Well said.' A voice behind him made him jump, and turning, he saw it was Brian. 'You've come a long way, speaking to my woodland realm like that,' he said.

'I came as soon as I could but if it hadn't been for them, I might have been too late.'

'Is that thing still looking for me?' gasped Oliver.

'No, it's been reduced to its basic elements and returned to the earth,' said Brian, casually. 'Actually more frightening than harmful, but what worries us more is what evil thing created it. So, we may be back to your unwelcome fellow guests from the portal.'

'If it was just a manifestation,' said Oliver, 'could it really have harmed me?'

'Oh yes,' said Brian, cheerfully, 'absolutely fatal to humans.'

'How very reassuring,' said Oliver, 'thank you so much.'

'Not at all,' said Brian, with a grin. 'Now where's that bird of yours?'

Oliver gave the summons and in an instant Lance was on his shoulder, his plumage a little ruffled and a pigeon feather sticking out of the corner of his beak. 'You called, Master,' he said, with a new note of respect in his voice.

'The danger's not over for your… Master,' said Brian, 'and now we've got to get him to the Speech House to meet his guide. Posthaste.'

'Change of plan?' said Lance.

'Driving him is too risky,' said Brian. 'Is there a portal near here?'

'You're joking!'

'You'll have to carry him.'

'Me? That's 'summon and instruct', serious necromancer stuff,' said Lance. 'Well above your garden grade, my fine rooted friend.'

'If you saw the authorisation I've got for this outing, you'd see that's nothing,' said Brian. 'I could turn you back into a magpie and not even have to account for it, even with your special powers. Or a feral pigeon, come to think of it.'

'Whoa,' said Lance, hurriedly. 'Of course, I'd be delighted to help.'

'Please prepare him,' said Brian, 'while I go and sort things out.'

'For what?' said Oliver apprehensively when he'd gone.

'You're to ride on my back,' said Lance. 'You'll like that.'

'Like hell I will!' shouted Oliver. 'I'm much too big!'

'In a minute,' said Lance patiently, 'Brian will be back with someone who can help you. Then I can get you to the Speech House, and you can get on with your journey.'

'I'm getting so tired of all this,' said Oliver, in a small voice.

'Most understandable,' said a deep, kindly voice, belonging to a venerable, white-bearded, elderly man, who appeared from nowhere, 'but needs must, I fear.' And with that he pressed both hands to Oliver's temples, until his world was spinning round and round.

'That should do it,' said Horace the Necromancer, peering down at the tiny figure. 'He'll be like that for half an hour. Any more than that and you'll need me again. *Bon voyage*, Oliver, or should we call you Olivetto? Ha, ha!'

'Lancelot, let me get him on your back and then off to the Speech House with you,' said Brian, in a tired voice. 'And brother, don't spare the feathers!'

8

When you're not used to being an inch tall, the world can be a daunting place. An ant the size of a cat is best avoided, it's difficult squeezing between huge blades of grass and everything smells like manure. But Oliver had little time to experience such a world before he found himself being plucked by a huge hand and placed in the feathers behind Lance's head. He clung there, sensing that this newly scaled-down world moved faster than his own, and that the distant, booming noise he was hearing was human speech.

Lance sprang from his perch, beat his wings in an ecstasy of power, and rose swiftly into the air. The wind tore at Oliver, the forest flashed past beneath them, and he clutched on, desperately, not daring to look down. Twenty minutes later they landed gently on a small wall near a hotel building in a forest clearing.

'Thank you,' said Oliver as he slid off the bird's back. He looked up at a fierce, yellow-rimmed eye, suddenly aware of what a hungry peregrine falcon could do to something his size, but Lance merely ducked his head, heaved himself upwards and flew away.

Dizzy and disoriented after the flight, Oliver sat down heavily on the ground and closed his eyes, and when he opened them a few minutes later, he found that he was back to his normal size. He sat up and looked around, and a slim, smartly dressed woman emerged from a large silver car parked nearby, smoothing her skirt, and smiled at him.

'How nice to see you, Oliver,' she said. 'Come along, we haven't much time.' She took him by the arm, and they walked towards the building, which, judging from a brass plate near the entrance, was a hotel called 'The Speech House'.

'Do you know why you're here?' she said.

'I was told it was to meet my next guide,' he said. 'Is that you?'

'Yes, I'm Myra. Didn't Meg say it might be me if she was called away?'

'I don't remember, there wasn't much time for chat when we met!'

'She did well, I heard, but then she was called away, leaving Brian to look after you, not to mention her van and your hawk.' She laughed. 'Typical of my sister Meg, dashing away like that, leaving us to pick up the pieces!'

'You're her *sister*!' he was astonished. 'But we met only this morning. So where is she now?'

'Probably prowling around in another dimension,' she laughed, 'in Ursus Minor as usual, seeing it's Saturday. We aren't very alike.'

'So you're not a morph.'

'No, fear! I'm much more frightening,' said Myra. 'And anyway, you don't need to know about me, not yet anyway. I'm sorry, but I've come at very short notice, and all I know is there's a clue to an important location here, which we need to find.'

'I don't think anyone's been well briefed on this part of my journey,' said Oliver.

'Well, let's see what we can find inside,' she said, and led him through a door into the dark interior of the house. They walked along an oak-panelled corridor, hung with hunting prints on the wall, and into a gloomy, high-ceilinged room with a sign saying 'Verderer's Courtroom' on its door. Inside was a low raised oak gallery, and a faded print on the wall depicting a long-barrow in a downland setting, called 'Wayland's Smithy.'

They found nothing else in the room to help them and so they returned to the picture.

"Do you know this place?' said Myra, pointing to the image of the burial mound.

'Wayland's Smithy?' said Oliver. 'I went there when I was very young, and found it *very* scary. I heard the locals thought it's haunted, and avoided it like the plague.'

'Is it near here?' said Myra.

'About forty miles away,' he said, 'on the other side of the River Severn.'

'I don't know your Earth as well as Meg does, but I can sense that place is a site of natural power. You're sure she didn't tell you anything else?'

'There was no time,' said Oliver.

Myra suddenly looked up and seemed to hear something. For a moment she looked worried and then said, 'I've got to leave you for a few hours. When you're alone try not to feel so anxious, your thoughts are like a beacon. I'll do something about that before I go.'

They returned to the car and once inside, Myra told Oliver to make himself comfortable, leaned over and touched his temples. Her image faded, her voice became faint and faraway and he slept. The next thing he knew was her shaking him awake, and a glance out of the car window showed him that it was dusk.

'I know now why we're here, but we must go quickly,' she said, starting the car.

'Go where?' he asked.

'To meet someone. I'll tell you more on the way.'

They left the car park and turned south towards the bridge crossing to England. On the way Myra said, 'I'm not surprised you're feeling anxious with what you've been through.'

'Brian's helped me feel less worried,' said Oliver, 'he's very reassuring.'

'A good, trusty ally,' said Myra. 'You must be puzzled about so many things, and you haven't had the chance to get the answers to a lot of questions. Can I help?'

'What exactly is this Shadow-side we're on?' said Oliver, 'I know it's similar, but not identical, to my own Earth, and contains some different things, but to me it seems so *real*.'

'If your journey teaches you anything,' said Myra, 'it will be about the nature of different 'realities'. Remember that to other cultures, you are still a primitive species, with no real insight into your own nature or understanding of the universe of which you are a part.

A recent species wedded to the primitive notion of a single 'reality.'

'Humanity's limited perception of reality has been around since Plato's story of moving shadows on a cave wall,' said Oliver, 'where the images perceived by humans as real are only a reflection of true 'reality.'

'And has knowing that *changed* anything for the human race?' said Myra.

'Perhaps not, but we've made great scientific progress,' said Oliver.

'Not much,' said Myra, 'in spite of your self-congratulation! You don't even know what makes up most of the matter in your own galaxy! But, to be fair, your best are *humble* creatures, for they know the more you learn, the more there is to understand. Like Newton's 'great ocean of truth' lying all undiscovered before him. And, in the words of another scientist, the universe is 'not only queerer than we suppose, but queerer than we *can* suppose.'

'What has all this to do with my question about the Shadow-side?' said Oliver.

'Everything,' said Myra, 'for to appreciate it you must abandon you*r* version of reality, and accept *different* 'realities', however strange they may seem!'

'Lord Sebastian told me that,' said Oliver.

'Because it's true,' said Myra. 'And bearing that in mind, you must now accept what I say, when I tell you that the Shadow-side contains what we call '*dream-reality.*' The embodiment of human imagining, produced during sleep.'

'You mean that there are things here because people *dreamt* about them?' said Oliver.

'Certainly, many things, living and… otherwise,' said Myra, 'but you will see only a fraction of what is here. And be content with that, for it is something no human has ever witnessed before.'

'What do non-humans make of this dream-reality?' said Oliver.

'It has been closely studied, but remains a mystery,' said Myra. 'Some believe it may be unique in the whole cosmos. And cynics think it's only in dreamlife that humans really come alive, for awake their lives are so dismal and trivial.'

'Sad but true,' said Oliver.

'Now to the matter in hand,' said Myra. 'The contest for Earth dominance is likely to result in a victory for artificial life, unless we can promote the Shadow-side for all its worth. Our position is that *if the gift of creative dreaming can be spread more widely throughout the galaxy, through an expanded portal network, we can help preserve the best of other cultures.* But to do this, natural life must dominate the Earth, for Artificials, barred from unaided access to portals, cannot offer to the star-ways such a gesture of goodwill.'

'So that's why humans were chosen to represent the future of all *natural* life,' said Oliver, 'but why me?'

'We don't know,' said Myra. 'Your innate ability to converse with animals may have helped. But whatever the reason, your meeting with Pierre was planned to coincide with Lord Sebastian's bid for natural life's dominance. The artificial side, led by Ovoid, responded immediately, and now both sides, locked in conflict, know that an inquiry will take place.'

'Why did I have to come to the Shadow-side?' said Oliver.

'Because, as I said, it's our trump card, and at the Inquiry you may be asked about it,' said Myra. 'And because you had to be *vetted* here. Don't forget you're representing both worlds.'

'Vetted by whom?' said Oliver.

'One day you may find out,' Myra smiled, 'but not from me.'

'So I passed muster?'

'Yes, or we wouldn't be talking now.'

'Myra, are you and Meg *spiritual* beings?'

'I suppose we are, in the sense that we're not permanently attached to bodies, such as yours,' she said, 'and not bounded by the natural laws of your universe.'

'Is Lord Sebastian like you?' said Oliver.

'No, he's quite different, he's a 'multiple being."

'Meaning?'

'Meaning what it says,' said Myra. 'If he chooses, he can co-exist and live simultaneously using any number of identical 'selves'. No more talking now, we need to keep focussed on our journey.'

It was getting dark as they cleared the great bridge over the Severn and headed east along the M4 motorway, leaving it at the Chippenham junction, and taking the Great West Road over the windswept hill past the White Horse at Cherhill. Descending into the Kennet valley, they sped on through what New Agers believed was a highly charged spiritual landscape near Avebury, where a roadworks sign directed them to turn off and follow a diverted route. They were alone on the small road, and after some time both of them began to feel uneasy.

The night was clear, stars shone brightly in the dark sky, and Myra drove slowly so as not to miss any signs. Then, without warning, the engine spluttered and died, and she steered the car into the side of the road. Oliver stopped dozing and, looking out of his window, noticed they'd reached a stretch of the road where it crossed a large gravel-pit filled with water. It was now very still and silent, and both of them felt the tension in the air.

'This isn't looking good,' said Myra. 'I'll take a look outside to see what's going on. Don't leave the car, Oliver.'

She got out of the car and held out her arm. Then Lance tumbled out of the night sky and perched on it with his head to one side. She whispered something to him, jerked her arm and he sprang away, whirling into the night. Before moving off into the darkness, she turned, smiled at Oliver and said she'd return soon.

It had been a long day, and in spite of his anxiety he fell asleep, until a sharp sound like a pistol shot jerked him awake. He focussed his eyes, and saw that thick ice was rapidly forming on the windows, zig-zagging crazily with a loud cracking sound. His heart thudding against his ribs, he strained his eyes to see through the rapidly icing window, frantically scanning the frozen lake. White fog was now rising up from its icy surface, casting a deathly white pall in the moonlight, and as its filmy layers thickened, the water vapour in the air itself seem to freeze.

Oh, Myra, Myra, *where are you?* thought Oliver. *Shield me from what's coming.* But what came wasn't what he was expecting, for it had a kind of staged beauty about it that the awful scuttling creatures he'd met before lacked. But it was no less deadly and frightening. For coming across the glittering ice towards him were three hooded figures in white, shining robes. As they drew nearer, they made no sound and seemed to *glide* along. Thirty metres away, their true nature was revealed for the nearest one raised its head, and for an instant Oliver saw a white, waxen face with but a single feature – a black, glistening mouth open and gaping, but void of teeth. And that was not all for as the figures seemed to *slide* towards him, so silently and smoothly did they move that Oliver, glancing down, saw beneath the swaying robe of the nearest one a single foot, moist and muscular, like that of a giant snail.

'*It's over!*' he thought, immobilised by the cold. He could only wait for what was to come, and he closed his eyes. He didn't want to fight anymore, or see anything ever again. Then memory flooded back and he uttered the summons. In an instant Lance was there, clawing for a hold on the frozen window-screen.

'Help!' shouted Oliver.

'Close your eyes and cover your ears,' cried Lance, who flew away, leaving a few feathers behind, as a clawed hand made a grab for him.

Oliver made a huge effort with his frozen hands, dimly aware of icy, bony fingers tearing at the glass to reach through, grasp and pin him to his seat. He felt nothing as the car began to tremble and shake as if in

97

the grip of a giant hand, nor did he see a huge flash followed by a mighty blast. All he was conscious of was whirling and twirling, turning and sliding down the dark sky, and after that, nothing.

***

He was lying on soft grass. Looking round, he wondered how many more times he was going to have to end up like this.

'Well done,' said a voice that seemed to come from a woody glade on a small hill away to his right. 'Hold on a moment, I'm getting a little stream organised over here. Then you can have a cooling drink.'

In a moment Oliver heard a plash and a gurgle, and saw a stream of clear water tumbling from a leafy bower towards him, between banks of fresh, green grass. He crawled to where the sparkling water created a bright little pool and, kneeling down, cupped his trembling hands into the water and drank thirstily. It tasted delicious, and revived him so completely that he sat back and calmly took in his surroundings.

In the clear sunny morning, he saw some distance away another grove of tiny, perfect trees, with the breeze gently stirring the aspens by the margin of a limpid pool. *Pretty, but ordinary enough*, he thought, but then he noticed the leaves were unfamiliar, and was the sky bluer than he was used to? And the grass greener? Pale yellow flowers were growing by the water's edge, and he bent to touch one, smelling its scent, which he found bewitching but unusual.

'Everything to your liking, I hope,' called the unseen voice.

'It's lovely here, and the water tastes delicious,' said Oliver, and then he remembered. 'What happened to me?' he cried. 'Am I dead?'

'Hold on a second,' said the voice, 'and I'll come over.'

In a few moments a fresh-faced, thick-set young man appeared from behind the bushes, wearing an open-necked shirt, a striped sports blazer, white trousers with wide bottoms and two-tone shoes. His wavy hair was long and shiny, he had a small moustache, and his bright blue eyes radiated boyish charm.

He smiled and offered his hand to Oliver, who had risen to his feet, and they both sat down. The affable stranger spoke first.

'I would say you're very much alive, wouldn't you?' he said.

'Just about,' said Oliver.

'Ah, nasty business, that,' said his host. 'Poor old Lance lost a few feathers. He was very put out.'

'Yes, I was worried about that,' said Oliver.

'And I hear the opposition nearly got to you again. But here you are safe. And here am I, ready and waiting to give you a warm welcome before Myra joins us. Did I get it right? Woods, trees, brook and flowers, all that kind of thing. Like the period kit?'

'Very nice, thanks,' said Oliver, 'very reassuring. Who are you, please?'

'Some humans call me Pan.'

'I thought you were a God of Antiquity.'

'Yes, I was, and I am,' said Pan. 'Sylvanus and Faunus to the Romans, but I prefer 'Pan'. It's easier for moderns, and you don't have jokes about having 'anus' in your name.'

'That must have been upsetting,' said Oliver, 'but here you are, Pan, alive and well, and making little streams flow.'

'Oh, I can do much more than that,' smiled Pan.

'Are you really here, or am I dreaming?'

'I don't know where you are,' said Pan, 'but I'm definitely here.'

'And what about Myra?' said Oliver. 'She left me in the car for a moment to look around and never came back. Do you know where she is now?'

'Who knows? They get around, those sisters,' said Pan. 'A billion years in the future, and a trillion light years away. All I know is that she or Meg will be here soon, and I don't relish falling down on the job of looking after you.'

'Well, at least she knew where to find me,' said Oliver, beginning to feel that another of his near-death experiences was not getting the attention it deserved.

Pan, detecting his chagrin, suggested a remedy. 'Would the company of a pretty nymph or two help to pass the time, before one of the sisters comes?' he said. 'You humans are partial to that sort of thing, aren't you?'

Much to his amusement, Oliver politely refused the offer and said that he'd just like to sit quietly by the brook and gather his thoughts. At that the God's face dropped a little, and he looked worried.

'Perhaps a few minutes,' he said, 'but we can't have you getting too *thoughtful*.'

'What's the problem?' said Oliver.

'It's all a question of *vibrations,*' said Pan, scratching his cheek. 'If you're mentally occupied it's harder for others to tap into your brain impulses and locate you. Vague thoughts make you mentally visible, and that means vulnerable.'

'Nothing can hurt me here, surely?' said Oliver.

'Not really, but we can't be too careful. Too much at stake, and we're not yet out of the wood,' said Pan. 'Talking of greenery, this is Arcadia, and there are some interesting creatures here you're due to meet. After your little nap, of course.'

'Very well,' said Oliver, looking around for a comfortable spot.

Pan nodded brightly. 'Right-ho. Look, if you don't mind I'll come back in my usual form. I'm not a natural morph like Meg, and it's a bit difficult keeping in shape, so to speak.'

He turned and walked briskly towards a nearby clump of trees and disappeared. Oliver sighed deeply. He sat watching a small fish making heavy weather of swimming upstream, and knew exactly how it felt. But, after a while, the soft music of the stream in that peaceful, cosy grove made him drowsy, and he stretched out in the dappled sunlight and fell into a deep sleep.

And as he slumbered in that lovely place, it seemed to him that all manner of creatures came to look at him and then steal away. Dryades first, dainty wood-nymphs and then their sisters, the Naiades, from the streams and lakes. Charming, shy and lithe; immortal, some said. And then a procession of fauns and satyrs, with human upper bodies and goat features below, and hefty centaurs, scowling, muscular men with horses' bodies. Even a shy unicorn took a quick look, and there was a rare visit from a winged horse, white and majestic, who could only have been Pegasus. And, of course, Pan was there, in his natural form: huge and amiable, red-faced and flat-featured, with two small horns on his head, and furry thighs and hooves like those of a huge beast.

It was Pan who let him sleep on, safely wrapped in his dreams, the god smiling when he saw the expressions of those who gazed at him, puzzled that such a little, timid creature like Oliver had been chosen for such a task. He waved them gently on and when, alone at last, he looked down at the tiny sleeping figure, he put a hand to his heart, and bowed with a look of great compassion. Should any of his wood-folk have seen it, they would not have thought him capable of such tenderness towards an interloper from a sullen, disbelieving world.

Visions flashed, steadied and dissolved in Oliver's mind as he lay asleep. And when he awoke he felt that each dream- visitor had brought something for him to keep. Nothing physical, but an intangible gift to help him on his way, be it foresight or cunning, cheeriness in the face of adversity, or dignity in the midst of ridicule. And when he awoke, sitting next to him was Myra, and Lance was on her arm.

'I can't take a lot more of this,' he said, smiling weakly at her. 'We humans aren't built to cope with all this… reality. We can only survive by looking at the shadows, and making up silly stories to comfort us in our isolation and loneliness.'

Myra smiled gently and said, 'Make friends with shadows and dreams, for your true nature as a life-form may be more dreamlike and less 'real' than you think. And your ultimate future as a species may lie there, even though, for the present, others of you may think otherwise. What is certain is that if you stay as you are, as a species you will only succeed within the limitations prescribed by your origins.'

'I'm afraid I'll let everyone down,' said Oliver. 'I know so little of other forms of natural life.'

'Pan will help you with that,' Myra said, 'and always remember there are good reasons why you have been given this task. And you are not alone – powerful allies like Brian and Lord Sebastian are by your side to help. You're making good progress, but there's more to learn, and not much time.'

'What's next?' he said.

'Being taught about the woodland realm by one of its greatest experts. Pan's away organising that, and as soon as he gets back, we'll see who he's found to be your tutor. And he or she will be the most important person in this part of your journey.'

9

When the god of Arcadia appeared, he was wearing the bemused air of one suffering from a surfeit of delight. Myra gave him a searching look and said, 'Well, Pan, who have you chosen to be Oliver's guide?'

He shifted uneasily and, avoiding her gaze, inspected his hooves with close attention. After scratching the grizzled hair on his chest for a while, he mumbled, 'Still *mulling* things over, my Lady, but nothing's… *crystallised* as yet.'

'You mean you *still* haven't found a tutor,' said Myra, acidly.

'Close, close…' he murmured, swishing his tail and arching his back, as if dislodging a troublesome fly.

Myra's eyes gleamed for a second and then she lost her temper. Her whole body began radiating light, and she seemed to grow until she towered above him. And as she raised her arm as if to strike him, there was a sudden whoosh and Meg appeared.

'Hello Myra,' she said, 'have I come at a bad moment?'

'Not for me, sister,' said Myra, 'but you may have saved Pan from one. Oliver requires guidance urgently, and our famous deity here was to find him a mentor versed in woodland ways. And what has he come up with? Nothing! But he still found time to get up to his usual tricks.'

'Happily,' said Meg, 'I have a solution that will please us all.'

'Which is?' said Myra.

'Now my son Wedros is free,' said Meg, 'and he's just *made* for the job.'

'Be serious, sister,' snapped Myra, 'this is important!'

Now it was Meg's turn to get angry, for as every species knows, criticism of a mother's son to her face is seldom without consequences. She drew herself up and faced her sister. 'You dare insult my child, and him a noble boy, with ichor flowing in his veins!' she shouted.

'Pretty thinly, I should think, my dear,' smiled Myra.

As Meg's fury grew so did her size, until it matched her sister's. Hissing, she clenched her fists, the sky darkened, and lightning played about the treetops. Oliver sought cover behind a nearby rock, followed closely by Pan, sweating with fear, a whole barnyard of odours pouring from his hairy flanks and woolly chest. Meanwhile the frightening sisters circled each other, as if in a knife fight.

'Great Zeus,' muttered Pan, 'I know who'll get it in the neck when this lot's over.'

'Ladies, ladies,' said a calm, rounded voice, 'let's not have this, and in front of our guest, too. You'll frighten him half to death.'

The sisters wheeled round to face the speaker.

105

'My dear sisters,' said Lord Sebastian, 'soon we will all face formidable foes, and to prevail we must pull together. No more of this, I implore you. And you two so fond of each other. Let me pour some soothing oil on these slightly troubled waters.'

Meg grinned and relaxed, and Myra managed a wintry smile.

'Pan agreed to find Oliver the best woodland guide to prepare him for his task,' said Myra.

'And doubtless he has been much exercised in securing a suitable candidate,' beamed Lord Sebastian.

'The 'exercise', my Lord,' said Myra, 'to which you delicately refer, has diverted his energies from him finding Oliver a tutor.'

'I offered the services of my son, Wedros,' said Meg. 'I thought it was the sort of job he would relish.'

'And one he would be admirably equipped to fulfil,' said Lord Sebastian.

'See... *sister*,' Meg gloated, 'dear Lord Sebastian agrees with me. When can he start?'

'Sadly, we cannot call on his services at present,' said Sebastian silkily, 'for he is attending a conference, many parsecs away, the details of which I am unable to reveal. A great honour for one so young.'

Both sisters began to smile, and a shaky harmony was returning to Arcadia.

'Do join us,' Sebastian said to Pan, peeping out from behind his rock, 'and tell us about your search for a tutor for Oliver.'

'With the help of Brian, the shrub spirit,' said Pan, who had anticipated the question, 'Oliver is deepening his ties with his woodland colleagues, both rooted and free. Of course, because of his fluency in their tongues, he's already more familiar with animal matters than with the woodland realm. And he maintains contact with avian life on Shadow-side in the shape of a peregrine falcon.'

'So what seems to be the problem?' said Sebastian.

'He needs to continue his woodland work in a more systematic fashion, at an advanced *practical* level,' said Pan, 'and a suitable mentor has proved hard to find.'

'Have you a candidate in mind?' asked Sebastian.

'Indeed yes, my Lord, a former protégé of mine, currently located on the other Earth.'

'I think I know who you mean,' said Sebastian. 'I thought he was a large *elf* when I first met him. Rather *lightweight* for a job like this, wouldn't you say, Pan?'

'My choice,' Pan replied, 'has lived a quiet, plant-friendly life, in sympathy with his sylvan clients. To achieve this *rapport,* he has not sought to flaunt his high intelligence, powers of endurance, and diplomatic skills. Strangers sometimes mistake this charming lightness of touch as a lack of personal *gravitas.*'

'You have approached him, I assume?'

'Yes, My Lord, and he's agreed to help, subject to concluding existing commitments,' said Pan. 'And, I propose we transit immediately to him to secure his services.'

'We?'

'I'll like Oliver to accompany me,' said Pan, 'for I'm sure his modest sincerity will be an asset in helping us 'clinch the deal', as our human friends would say.'

'Be quick about it then, but 'clinch' *discreetly*,' urged Sebastian.

Pan turned to Oliver with a smile, and they were about to leave when, with a loud crash, a monstrous quadruped swept onto the scene. Oliver had already met Wedros, and recalled the centaurs' reputation as ill-mannered, bad-tempered bullies, but close up and in the flesh, this one was truly terrifying.

Lord Sebastian, as always, summed up the situation in a flash. 'Wrach, my dear fellow,' he said mildly to the huge animal rearing above him, its grizzled features twisted in a ferocious scowl, 'what an unexpected pleasure! Why, it seems like Earth millennia since we last met.'

'I'm not here by choice,' snarled the centaur, 'but now I am, that bitch over there,' pointing a grimy hoof at Meg, 'can tell me where I can find my son, after she left him to whirl around a fucking piss-poor lump of rock like Earth, shifting shitty human space debris.'

'Don't you come here making trouble, you loathsome piece of cosmic horse-shit,' Meg screamed. 'And where were you for his terrible twenty thousands, when he needed a father?'

'Not around, luckily for the boy,' said Myra.

'And you can keep out of this, you mad harridan,' said Wrach, wheeling round and raising both forefeet in the air.

My God, thought Oliver, *what a frightening beast he is!*

'That's enough of that,' said Pan, stepping forward, suddenly grown in stature and authority, now truly godlike, with unfeigned power and authority. Wrach snorted, but stood down, breathing hard.

'My dear Wrach,' said Sebastian, 'by great good fortune, as I was just telling the ladies, I have secured a place for Wedros in a conference of great importance. Far removed from his now admirably completed task of revolving around a modest planet, I do assure you.' He paused and smiled at Wrach, and there must have been something in his gaze that unnerved the centaur.

'Well, alright,' he muttered, backing off, 'that's more like it.'

'Please tell us as to what alerted you to our presence here today,' said Sebastian, gently.

'I was minding my own business in the forest,' said Wrach, 'when this hawk flew down from nowhere and told me to come here. Then a treebeing turned up, found a local portal, and I was transported here.'

'A 'tree-being', you say,' said Sebastian, 'with branches and foliage? Things like that?'

'More like some poncey Park Ranger,' snorted Wrach, 'you know how these wood spirits get above themselves. But I can smell 'em coming a mile away. Had a big dog with him, too, handsome brute.'

'Did the bird say anything else?' said Myra.

'Told me to say he was coming to see you,' said Wrach, 'you might need some help with 'heavy lifting,' and me and my boys might fit the bill. Don't know what that's about.'

'He meant that you might help us overcome various difficult *physical* problems we may soon encounter,' said Lord Sebastian.

'Like a bit of *enforcing*, you mean?'

'You'd enjoy that,' said Meg, winking at her sister.

'We like to keep in shape, if that's what you mean,' Wrach said, flicking his tail, 'don't see why I should though. Still, you helped the boy. And who's he?' he added, pointing at Oliver.

'A visitor from the parallel world,' said Pan, 'on a study tour to the woodland realm.'

'Oh, yes,' said Wrach.

'Right, that's all settled then,' said Sebastian, 'and if we need a bit of *practical* help, my dear Wrach, I take it we can call on you and your colleagues. There'll be ambrosia for all, when the hard work's done.'

'Wouldn't say no,' mumbled the centaur, backing up, and preparing to go. 'You know where to find me, and I'll put the word around that you'll need us 'herd-handed'. If you want me to show the little fellow over there a few things, let me know.'

Wrach galloped away, and Lord Sebastian turned to the others and said, 'It's time you two contacted Oliver's advisor. Time's getting short.'

'For what?' Oliver asked

Lord Sebastian looked vague and murmured that time was always snapping at their heels, and began musing about Father Time, whose father was the most boring entity he'd ever met. His reminiscence was interrupted by the arrival of Brian, dressed in a khaki outfit, with Lance on his arm and Pierre at his heels. The dog was beside himself with joy at seeing Oliver.

'We'll be off, then,' said Pan, cheerfully. 'Wish us luck, everybody.'

Pierre gave a muted howl, but apart from that they left in a rather strained silence.

***

Pan beckoned to Oliver as they walked away from the others along the side of the stream. 'Fact is, my friend,' said Pan quietly, looking back over his shoulder, 'fact is… I know who's best to help you, but it's a bit tricky getting to him.'

'What's the problem?"

'As I said, he seemed willing to help, but I can't reach him. He doesn't answer my e-mail.'

'You use *e-mails*!' said Oliver.

'Ethereal Messaging!' said Pan. 'And that's why we need to go to see him using a portal, but I'm a bit *approximate* at getting the timing right. And pinpointing the location's not my strong suite, either.'

Now he tells me, thought Oliver, who said, 'What's the name of this tutor anyway?'

'Roland,' said Pan. 'At least, that's the one he uses on the other Earth. He's the Galaxy Advisor on cactaceae, rocky planet specialist for woodland studies, 'go-to' chap on wood-wide web, herb consultant and fungus specialist. Understands all their languages and most of their secrets.'

'Not Roland *Chilvers* – I know him!' said Oliver. 'He was our neighbour at home, and he helped us transit.'

'That should help us get a fix on him, and save me a lot of grief,' said Pan, with a huge sigh of relief. 'Now I feel *much* better. Oh, is that not an old friend of mine

I see by that brook there, where the naiads bathe about this time? Back in a jiffy.'

Oliver walked slowly to where they'd all gathered, but everyone had gone. He sat down and thought about the future, but things didn't look too promising. After half an hour Pan returned in human form, breathing heavily, with wet hair. He was wearing a leather jacket, red trousers and two-tone golf shoes.

'Come on,' he said, 'time to go!'

'I've been waiting to do just that,' said Oliver, irritably.

'In Arcadia,' said Pan, with an edge to his voice, 'we go when I'm ready. Don't worry, as soon as we find the portal, we'll work out the password, and get the time setting sorted. We'll be with Lord Roland in no time.'

They were walking on a hillside through the most delightful countryside, green, fresh and fragrant, gently perfumed from some unseen blossom. Below them Oliver saw a pool of murky water, and a slight breeze ruffled the delicate fronds of the mimosa-like trees clustered around its margin. When they reached it there was a flurry and a splashing, but nothing to be seen except for widening ripples in the water.

'More of your naiads, I suppose,' said Oliver.

'No, they keep to streams of fresh water,' said Pan, 'and keep away from still waters like this. They're very old and get stagnant, and the things that live down there, under the banks, are ancient blighters, and ugly as sin. Not my cup of tea at all, but I'm still responsible for them, just like everything else in Arcadia.'

'I thought all the things here, the woods, plants and… beings, lived together in complete harmony,' Oliver said.

'Once, maybe,' said Pan, 'but everything changes, and we don't have the same control over some of the creatures we're sent now. All sorts get foisted on us, and no-one seems willing to *restrict* the numbers like they used to. When I complain they say, 'Pan, that's old thinking, reach out, be inclusive.' And I tell them my thoughts and feelings might be old and a bit threadbare, but there's still plenty of wear left in them!'

'Do you know where we'll find the portal?' said Oliver.

'More or less.'

'Is there anyone we can ask to help if we can't find it?' said Oliver.

'*What* a good idea,' said Pan, 'especially for some poor bugger like me who should know everything, as D-in-C of the entire Woodland Realm.'

'What's that?'

'Deity-in-Charge,' what else? Not very bright, you humans, are you?'

'I might not be too clever, but at least I know where to find the portal,' said Oliver, hotly.

'Good for you,' said the god, grinning.

'Seriously, Pan,' said Oliver, 'the deeper I get involved, the more confused I get. It seems so unreal, and I wonder if it's all just happening in my head, and I'm dreaming it all up.'

'It will be real enough in its consequences for you humans,' said Pan, 'as you'll find out if we don't win. Anything in particular you've found really odd?'

113

'Well, the Controller, for one.'

'Oh, him,' said Pan. 'Got to take Ovoid with a pinch of salt.'

'I do – I've never believed in all that stuff anyway,' said Oliver.

'Quite right,' said Pan. 'He'd like others to think he governs the entire cosmos, and he's not even Senior Controller in the local group of fifty-four galaxies, because I know him. Ovoid's only the Controller of your galaxy, for what it's worth. There are *millions* of others like him in your universe alone, not to mention those in the parallel ones some claim exist.'

'Do they?' said Oliver.

'Look, I'm only a woodland god, how would I know?'

'But our galaxy's pretty big, isn't it?'

'Nothing to get excited about. Usual big black hole in the middle, and a few hundred billion stars and planets.'

'Seems huge to me, Pan,' said Oliver. 'Oh dear, it's all getting too much for me again.'

'You'll cope,' said Pan. 'Don't forget you've been brought in from scratch at the highest level of terrestrial policy.'

'But I still have difficulty in sorting out what's real or not.'

'I thought the others put you right about all that 'what is reality' stuff?' said Pan. 'For the record, I'll add my tuppence-worth. Is 'real' something you can see and touch? Your senses are telling you that. What is matter? You haven't a clue. And 'thoughts' may simply be vibrations. And what of dreams? The stuff you're made of? Can't they be as real as anything else? The only reality you need to face, my dear human, is to 'get real' and stop analysing your feelings, because you're not very good at it! You're not mentally equipped to understand some things, and it's boring! Now can we get on!'

'When the sisters were quarrelling,' said Oliver, past caring, 'and we sheltered behind a rock, I spotted some marks on it, like the ones outside the portal we first used.'

'Excellent,' said Pan, greatly relieved.

They retraced their steps and Oliver pointed out the script. 'Can we go straight to the other Earth from here?' he said.

'Yes,' said Pan, 'and back to where you and Roland lived. Hopefully. Looking at these ancient marks, we'd be lucky to get to the right *era.*'

'Now what's wrong?'

'What we've got here, my friend, is an ancient portal,' said Pan bitterly, 'probably reconditioned and then dumped here because someone in Portal Central thinks we're just a bunch of bucolic stumblebums who wouldn't notice.'

'What now?'

'We'll give it a go but remember it's a cranky old machine and a certain *precision* might be lacking in its timing controls. 'When' we'll end up at first is anyone's guess. Great Zeus, what I'd give for a nice swim-about with a few naiads, followed by a nice relaxing massage from a nymph. Right now. Where are these people when their god needs them?'

10

'Oliver, what did Roland do when he opened your portal?' said Pan, looking closely again at the incisions on the rock. 'It's been a while since I did this.'

'He touched the marks on the tomb wall,' said Oliver, 'and said something about 'runes' and 'rhythms.''

'Yes, yes,' cried Pan, 'it's all coming back.' He turned to the rock, stroked the marks and chanted, 'O runes with your rhythms as old as the sky, now let these words help me to open the eye.' For a while nothing happened, and then a line appeared in the rock and grew into a rectangle the size of a door, and a dark aperture filled in the outline. The god intertwined his fingers and cracked the joints like a safe-breaker preparing for a job. He grinned. 'You never lose your touch,' he said. 'Now let us begin – remind me where you began your transit, and we can start there. And then, with a bit of luck, we can contact Roland Chilvers.'

'Will the portal take us anywhere we want to go?' said Oliver.

'You know,' said Pan. 'In the early days you had to almost shout at the thing to get it to go where you wanted. But things have moved on, and now all you do is *think* of something or someone at a particular time, and you'll go there. Of course, it still only responds to whoever opened the door, or someone they have nominated to instruct it. And the directions must be *precise*, or goodness knows where they'll end up.'

'Quite simple then,' said Oliver, no longer surprised at finding that what at first glance seemed straightforward was much more subtle. He thought for a moment and then said, 'Can anyone open a portal and use it?'

'Of course not,' said Pan. 'I only just qualify to 'command' a portal, and as a Deity of Antiquity, I'm a 'second-level Spirit.''

'I've never heard of spiritual levels,' said Oliver.

'Really? You don't know about the Seven Planes of Existence?'

'No,' said Oliver, 'what are they? What level are humans, and Meg and Myra? What about Lord Sebastian?'

'Mankind's probably lumped in with plants and animals, about level one, I should think,' said Pan, 'although I've never seen a human as powerful as a fine oak, or as beautiful as a rose. I've no idea about Sebastian, but the girls move at will through space and time, so I'd put them between high two and low three. And Roland might be even higher, for he's responsible for woodland species on umpteen star systems.'

'Do you think they'll expect me to know more about all that at the Inquiry?' said Oliver.

'No idea,' said Pan, frowning, 'but I know a man who does. Hold on a moment and I'll ask him.' He closed his eyes and they both stood in silence for a minute or two.

'He's coming down,' said Pan.

'Who?' said Oliver.

'Someone you've already met,' said Pan.

'Where's he coming from?'

'I don't know,' said Pan vaguely, looking longingly towards the pool where the naiads bathed at that time of day. 'The Athens Academy, I expect, or the Lyceum. Ask him. He's here now.'

Oliver looked up as the white robed figure of the Necromancer came around the rock and joined them.

'Good day to you both,' he said, beaming at Oliver. 'None the worse for your *aerial* adventure, I'm pleased to see.'

'How nice to see you again, Sir,' said Oliver.

'Now what can I do for you two young beings?' he said.

'Meister Horace,' said Pan, 'as you know, Oliver will represent all terrestrial living beings at The Cosmic Inquiry. But he's never heard of the Spiritual Levels. We want him to show the judge that humans can transcend their humble origins, and so we wondered if he should know more about the subject?'

'And you sought guidance from me,' smiled Horace. 'From *me*. A jobbing peddler of party tricks, a poor entertainer of gimcrack legerdemain, a shabby…'

'Yes, yes, Meister,' said Pan, 'please, do us the honour of an explanation.'

'Oho, an 'honour,' you say? What a compliment. Something I hardly warrant, my dear Pan,' said Horace. 'Any *honorarium* involved would be mine, indeed.'

'But what is your *answer*, Meister Horace?' said Oliver.

'No use at all,' said the Necromancer, briskly. 'Most beings happily go about their lives in total ignorance of higher levels of consciousness. Start worrying them with other realities they can't ascend to without dying, or which they couldn't understand even if you explained it to them, and it's not going to help them or anyone else.'

'So that's it, is it?' said Oliver. 'You know, Meister, I'm not sorry to hear that.'

'You're moving on,' smiled Horace, 'you have seen that acceptance is sometimes better than the fruitless pursuit of the unknowable. Just as love is greater than prayer,' he added. Moving towards Oliver, he put a hand on his shoulder and looked deeply into his eyes. 'You'll learn more about the Spiritual Levels later if you need to, and are better able to cope with the knowledge. '

Oliver said nothing but smiled, and in that tranquil moment, even Pan fell silent, as if feeling, for an instant, the rare peace that eludes even a god of Arcadia, immersed in the problems of his realm. Merely a shadow world of imagination to some, but all too real for him.

Horace smiled again, and said to Oliver, 'Farewell. We'll meet again before too long.' And to Pan he said, 'You were right to summon me. Allow me a word of advice – although you and I disarm others with our foolishness, I know when to stop. How you remind me of Zeus, my dear boy, and what great friends we were, your father and I.'

He walked and disappeared behind the rock, and there was a long silence as Oliver and Pan recovered from the encounter. At last Oliver cleared his throat and said, 'About the portals. I travelled between the two Earths, but only remember using a portal once. Why was that?'

'No idea,' said Pan. 'Meg or Myra might know.'

'And you're from the shadow world, Pan, but you can live on my Earth, or we wouldn't be going there. How's that possible?'

'*You* survive in Arcadia, and you're not even a minor god,' said Pan. 'No more questions now, it's time to go, and when I've activated it I'll tell the portal to respond to your thoughts. When we get inside, think hard about where you began your first transit and *will* us to go there.'

Pan manipulated the runes, the portal door opened, and they walked inside. Oliver closed his eyes and tried hard to visualise the tomb in the cemetery, and after a pause the aperture closed and the journey began. But this time, instead of the gentle motion Oliver was expecting, the portal bumped and bucked violently, accompanied by an ominous grating noise as it twisted and turned. There was a violent crash, and then silence.

'Takes me back to the old days, this portal. It should be in a museum, or a scrapyard,' said Pan, rubbing his back where he'd been thrown against the wall. 'I'll not even open the door, I just know we're nowhere near where we want to be. Are you sure you're *concentrating*?'

'Yes, I am!' said Oliver indignantly, redoubling his mental efforts. That seemed to work, and after another roller-coaster ride they came to rest with a thump. 'Journey's end,' he said, triumphantly.

'Not too sure about that,' said Pan, and told the portal to open its door. Outside Oliver caught a glimpse of a reeking swamp, bathed in a dirty, yellow light, with huge ferns arching into a leaden sky. A blast of humid air, laden with foul gas bubbling up from rotting vegetation beneath the scum-covered water, surged into the portal.

'Late Carboniferous period at a guess,' he said, 'not *quite* my era.'

'I'll have a look around and try to get some bearings,' said Pan. 'One of my larger animal forms, I think.' He slipped outside, and Oliver saw him changing and expanding as the entrance closed. He waited impatiently and then the aperture was wrenched open and Pan appeared, all bulk, hooves and horns, wrestling with a monstrous creature. He threw it down with a mighty effort, and crashed into the portal, instantly reverting to human size and shape as he did so.

'What on Earth was that?' said Oliver.

'A myriad, not the brightest, but handy with its claws,' said Pan, inspecting a lacerated thigh.

'Could you see where we are?'

'Difficult to say,' said Pan, 'no-one around capable of speech. If you ask me, life's rather *primitive* around here. What they need is a god, and a bit of discipline. Maybe I'll come back one day and see if there's an opening. Only part-time, though.'

'We'll never see Roland at this rate,' lamented Oliver.

'Don't despair,' said Pan, 'I've just remembered that if it's only a *person* you want to see, things are simpler, because transiting depends on mental constructs.'

'Like 'thoughts',' said Oliver.

'The very word, 'recollected,' of course.'

'You mean 'memories.''

'You're good at this, aren't you?'

'Not really,' said Oliver. 'So if I was in control of the portal, *remembered* Roland and directed it to him, it would take us to him.'

'Yes, if you really concentrated.'

'So, what are we waiting for?'

'*We* are waiting for you to do what you say – think of Roland, wish to be with him, and speak the words.'

'What words?'

'The words that will come to you if you do what I've just told you to do,' said Pan. 'Really, Oliver, anyone would think you didn't want this thing to work.'

Oliver, fighting down his irritation, thought hard about Roland in his suburban living room, trying to forget he was a naturist. Then a voice in his head said 'Humpty dumpty,' and the portal began moving. And this time they ended up at dusk in a sunken lane running through pleasant, neatly farmed countryside. And judging from the metalled road and telephone wires in the distance, they were in England, and near the time period for which they were looking.

'No sign of Roland, and nothing I recognise around here,' said Oliver, looking around. 'Where are we?

'Search me,' said Pan. 'I'll go outside and find a local to help, someone more intelligent than the last lot.'

'Don't forget we're not in Arcadia now,' said Oliver.

'True enough,' said Pan. 'Perhaps it's best that I make contact with some non-human life-forms. I suggest you wait here for a moment – some animals can be a bit *touchy* about humans.'

Oliver nodded and, after Pan had disappeared, looked around. He saw he was standing in what must be an ancient way, bisecting the undulating wooded countryside like a scar, the deeply sunken track overshadowed by ugly stunted trees and tough thorny shrubs, with coarse grass growing high between the gaps. In the midst of such an attractive landscape, this twisting, hidden path had a forbidding feel, as if cursed by an evil past. In the gathering dusk, Oliver felt uneasy there, and waited impatiently for Pan's return.

When he did appear, Pan seemed unusually anxious, for his local contact had revealed that there was something very wrong with their arrival – as if the portal had been deliberately *directed* there. He didn't know how that was possible, but all the local natural life, sensing danger, had sought refuge underground or taken to the hills.

'What are you saying?' cried Oliver.

Pan said it was getting worse, for the portal wasn't responding. That meant they couldn't leave, and as he felt Oliver was in grave danger, he needed to organise his protection. He urged him not to worry, for he'd put a forest shield around him. But now he had to change his shape. 'Look away if you don't like wolves,' he said, 'and don't forget Lance. I'll also send someone to keep you company.'

Oliver turned away and when he looked again Pan was gone, but in his place was a large barn owl sitting on a stump next to him. 'Hello Oliver,' it said.

'Am I protected?' said Oliver.

'You've got a forest shield around you,' said the bird. It keeps mosquitos away, but if what I've heard is on the way, you'll need a sight more than that.'

'What's coming?'

'An Eldritch.'

'What's that?' said Oliver, hoping it was not as frightening as it sounded.

The owl shifted uneasily, and said that in the library where he'd once nested, he'd seen an open book in the reading room about them. 'Superior owls, like me,' it said, 'memorise text easily,' and it quoted a passage about Eldritches. According to the text, they were 'ancient horrors, solitary and rarely seen by man. Huge and frightful to look at, they dwell in the unreachable places of great forests, swamps or deserts. American Indians say they carry the stench of death and decay with them, and speak of them only by day, never when the shadows lengthen. For they hunt by night, growing more powerful the longer they live.'

'A bit *dramatic* for this part of the world, don't you think?' said Oliver.

'There's more if you'd only let me continue,' said the bird, and quoting again from memory, it said, 'They hate mankind, and if one senses a man alone it takes off and, flying at great speed, swoops down on him like a vast bird of prey, clamping him in its great talons, sharp as razor wire. It then forces him to run beside it in great bounds until his feet are bloodied and misshapen, before dragging him up into the air where its headlong flight forces tears of blood from his eyes. Its claws leave deep scars on his broken body, which is discarded, and dropped to earth, scarcely alive, the man driven insane with pain and shock.'

Oliver rather wished the pedantic owl had kept quiet, for it was now quite dark, and a cool breeze was wafting through the leaves. There was still no sign of Pan. And then he heard a heart-stopping 'whoosh,' as if a powerful gust of wind had passed through the branches of the trees above.

'It's come!' screamed the owl, and disappeared. Oliver, shaking with fear, huddled down with his back to a tree, holding in front of him a broken branch, all he had to ward off what was coming. A huge, black, misshapen mass, high up in the trees, like a huge, emaciated vampire bat, its eyes shining and mouth moving slightly, was glaring around, searching the ground below. Oliver knew in an instant that it was too late for flight, as the great creature lifted itself off the branch and swept towards him, crashing down through the branches.

Oliver shrieked the summons and found his lips saying the words of power as great talons tore into his flesh, and he was lifted up and carried away over the trees to level ground, where the creature began dragging him along the ground, faster and faster. He gasped, screaming with pain as he frantically twisted and wriggled like a worm on a hook, trying to loosen the embedded needle claws. Tearing along, now in huge bounds, he felt his feet burning… burning, and, as the creature took to the air, he felt his back clamped in a terrible vice, for its talons were taking his whole weight.

The pain was so intolerable that Oliver missed the scream of friction as a streak of blinding light, like a stream of molten gold, shot through the darkening sky like a meteor. Something hit the Eldritch with a clap like thunder and Oliver fell to earth amid a flurry of scales, teeth, entrails and splintered bone. He lay there in agony, raw pain invading every part of his body, face and hands burned, back lacerated and scalded, flesh-peeled feet pouring with blood.

And then Pan was there, beside himself with rage and remorse, and Horace the Necromancer, too. The cool, comforting hand of the kindly man was on his forehead. The light faded and he went to a place beyond the reach of pain.

11

Pan and Horace decided it would be best to transfer Oliver from the scene of the attack on his birth world to a 'safe house' on the Shadow-side. They moved rapidly, and Horace stayed with him to make sure Oliver was comfortable. Meanwhile Pan took up the search for Roland, and handling their same portal, this time with great skill, quickly tracked him down. Arriving at the cemetery by the River Thames at nightfall, he assumed a human shape and made his way to the Chilvers' house. He knocked on the front door and Roland appeared, wearing a dressing gown that had seen better days.

He looked warily at the large, weather-beaten, ruddy-faced man dressed in a thick trawlerman's pullover, wearing what looked like waders over thick moleskin trousers. 'Can I help you?' he said, looking over his shoulder to make sure Doris was safe in the kitchen.

'Have I changed so much you can't recognise me?' Pan said.

'Yes, you have,' said Roland, shortly. 'Who are you?'

There was a brief flash while Pan revealed his true identity to his former protégé and then resumed his human form.

'What's up?' said Roland. 'I was just getting dressed to go to bed.'

'It's about Oliver,' said Pan, 'the human I told you about.'

'I remember,' said Roland. 'Sebastian told me about him.'

'I didn't know that,' said Pan.

'Said I was to drop everything to help the lad. Chop, chop! Utmost importance.'

'He's been attacked again,' said Pan, 'and this time it's serious. He's so weak and badly injured, we might lose him.'

'Not again!' said Roland. 'If this is because you've let him out of your sight for a single second….'

'Or let something evil transit with him in the first place,' snapped Pan, 'this attack might not have happened. Anyway, he's safe on Shadow-side now.'

'Give me a moment to think up some travelling clothes,' said Roland, 'and then take me to him. No fuss, though – we'd better just use the local portal.'

When they arrived, after a rapid transit, they found Oliver in bed, with Lance perched above him. For the briefest moment Roland stiffened when he saw the frail, white-haired invalid, and then he said, 'You look as if you've been in the wars since I last saw you, young man.'

'Merely attacked by an Eldritch,' said Oliver, 'nothing serious, nothing I can't handle.' He then burst into tears.

128

'What saved him?' said Roland, quietly aside to Pan.

'Sensibly, you called Lance, didn't you?' said Pan, bending down to comfort Oliver. 'And he summoned a Draco. Not authorised to do that, of course, but what a piece of work they are! Built like a dreadnought, and armoured like a…'

Roland threw him a glance of such glacial reproach for these loose words that the god almost cringed before him. It was a glimpse of huge, reserved power, and, in spite of his anguish, Oliver felt relieved. For here was someone he'd greatly under-estimated, and even Sebastian could not have displayed authority so convincingly.

'He's lost a few toes, and has third-degree burns,' whispered Pan to Roland miserably.

'Pan, you come with me,' said Roland, and when they were out of earshot he turned on him. 'If you were misbehaving when the boy needed you most,' he said, 'Sebastian will hear of it, and we'll have you stripped of every power and vestige of authority you've ever possessed.'

'I swear I only left Oliver for a moment to contact locals to protect him, my Lord,' Pan protested, 'and I can easily prove it. But let's leave inquests for now, it's more important for Horace to help him recover.'

'Very well, use the Ethereal Way if you need it,' said Roland. 'Here's the code. After you've seen it, remember to forget it.'

They returned to the invalid. 'Please don't expect too much of me,' Oliver cried, the tears flowing down his face.

'My dear, brave little human,' said Roland without a hint of patronage, bending down and speaking softly, 'you've suffered much, but you will soon feel better. Now rest for the moment.' He laid his hand on Oliver's forehead, and he went out like a light.

Roland straightened up and looked at Pan. 'I don't like it,' he said. 'These attacks are getting worse. This won't be the last, and the next may prove fatal. Oliver's experience makes him more valuable now, so they'll try harder and we must be doubly vigilant. I'll speak to Sebastian – we must decide about alerting our reserve. Please look after poor old Oliver, and try not to screw anything up!'

***

One of Horace's many callings had been that of 'physician', and he relished the opportunity to practise his craft. His apprenticeship had included clinical diagnosis, pharmaceutical remedy and a dash of surgery. His knowledge of drugs and herbs was unsurpassed, far eclipsing even his reasonable diagnostic skills, but his skill as a surgeon, judging from the reaction of its recipients, came a very poor third. Happily, Oliver's injuries, although severe, were those best suited to Horace's talents, and he made rapid progress under his care. He was heavily sedated for much of his time in bed, and the lack of conscious pain, and the use of clever dressings and powerful drugs, led to rapid infection-free healing.

Roland had spoken to Sebastian, who was concerned by the setback to their schedule. No date had yet been set for the Inquiry, but he was sure that sometime soon they would be pressed to agree one. He gave Horace three weeks to restore Oliver to health, before they stood him down in favour of his replacement.

When Roland next visited him, two weeks had passed. Oliver had continued to make good progress in the capable hands of nurses who, in spite of modern approaches to care, for some reason wore Victorian uniforms. And Lord Sebastian had sent his best wishes, which was most unusual.

'Where's Pan?' Oliver asked.

'He went back to Arcadia,' said Roland, 'but he's on hand the moment we want him.

'Is Arcadia near here?' said Oliver.

'I can't tell you that,' said Roland. 'All you need to know is you're in a safe place. The less about where that is, the lower the risk of something picking up your thoughts.'

'Does anyone know what happened to the portal we were using the day I was attacked?'

'Sebastian's people couldn't figure out what affected the controls of your portal, or why Pan's shield was ineffectual,' said Roland. 'Great power was involved, but what it was or who it belonged to is unknown. What's certain is that it was a very well-planned attempt to harm you, and Sebastian's anxious for you to keep on the move. I'm sorry, but we must press on as soon as you feel able.'

'I understand, of course,' said Oliver, 'but do you think you could please take me home, even if it's only for a moment? To when everything was more...

familiar, when my brother was around, and Molly and I were getting to know each other. I'm not asking to meet them, it's just to help me get my bearings.'

Roland looked doubtful, and said he'd need to take advice on that. He left the room and came back smiling. 'The visit to your birth-side home has been agreed,' he said, 'as long as it's short and doesn't include any interaction with family or friends. And we're to travel by portal, which won't attract any undue attention. I'll return in a week, when I'm sure you'll be fit and ready to go.'

Horace was advised about the plan and now added mystical remedies to his more conventional treatment of Oliver's injuries. As a result, when Roland returned, as promised, Oliver had regained much of his usual health, and considerably more energy than before the attack.

Roland and Oliver left the house, turned into a small alleyway and stood in front of a wall on their right. Oliver assumed it contained a portal and was not surprised when, after Roland had uttered the words, the familiar outline of an aperture appeared. Before they got in he said, 'We'll arrive in the cellar of the Lamb and Limpet, at dusk. Around the time you transited.'

'What a brilliant idea,' said Oliver, smiling for the first time.

With Roland in charge, the ride in the portal was swift and the landing smooth and gentle. When the door opened, they were in a cellar, with the reassuring noises of shoes clumping on wooden floorboards and the murmur of conversation from above. Oliver climbed the wooden stairs that led up to the floor behind the bar, levered open the trap-door, and looked around. It was early evening, and only a few locals were around. The reserve barman, Fred, was in the snug, collecting glasses, and with Roland behind him, they crept along behind the bar and out through the back door. They walked around the corner, came into the pub from the front door, and found a quiet table. Roland went to the bar and ordered some beer, and nobody noticed them as they drank their pints.

'Frank and Cynthia are safe in Brittany, I think they rather like the place,' said Roland. 'Molly's still looking after some kittens, but they're not intended for the witch trade, and Doris is keeping an eye on her. Adrian's back to his old self and still keen on Molly, but as you know, she's only interested in you.'

'Hearing all that makes me feel so much better,' said Oliver, stretching out his legs. 'And a decent pint of Wreaker's inside me, as well.'

'You've been out of commission for a bit so let's review how you got this far and what's going on now,' said Roland, 'then we can see what's in store for you.'

'Sounds like time for another pint!' said Oliver, grinning.

When Roland returned from the bar with the drinks, he continued his summary. 'When you met Pierre in the lay-by it was a signal for Doris and I to become 'activated', he said. 'Your cat Cain, who had special powers, aware of impending danger, met Yvonne and Yvette, who guided you to the portal. Following the surprise attack on the cats, you and Pierre were transited to the Shadow-side earlier than planned, with Malesch and Vormint illegally 'side-gating' with you in the portal. There you met Lord Sebastian, in the 'hotel,' where you also met Wedros and observed Ovoid. Since then you've been guided by Meg, Brian and Lance, Myra and Pan, and with their help warded off three deadly assaults mounted by your rivals.'

'It makes me tired just hearing about it!' smiled Oliver.

'Remember that they've recently thrown very nasty things at you, but to no avail!' said Roland. 'And nor will they – at least, not on my watch!'

'Oh, that's alright then!' said Oliver.

'Seriously, it's reassuring how much the opposition fears you,' said Roland, 'and with your growing experience, you'll be even more of a threat in the future.'

'I'm so frightened most of the time,' said Oliver. 'They seem so much more powerful than us.'

'You're coping well, but you're bound to feel anxious and weak after your injuries,' said Roland. 'So now I'm going to ignore my instructions to whisk you back to Shadow-side, and suggest you come home with me, see Doris, and get a good night's sleep. And tomorrow we'll plan the next part of your journey.'

12

Oliver was more cheerful at breakfast than he felt, for he was only slightly better after his night's sleep.

'Thanks for letting me reach home,' he said to Roland. 'I suppose now it's back to the Shadow-side.'

'Change of plan,' said Roland. 'Bit of a flap at the other end when we didn't get back last night. I was bawled out by Sebastian, but he wants us to carry on with your training here, as long as we keep a low profile.'

'I'm sorry you got into trouble on my account,' said Oliver, 'but I'm raring to go on now.'

They went into the study and sat down at his large partner's desk.

'Before we start, do you have any questions?' said Roland.

'Are you really the Director of Galactica Woodlandia?' asked Oliver.

'So they tell me,' he grinned.

'How many planets do you look after?'

'How many are there in your galaxy, do you think?'

'Several million, at least.'

'Eight hundred billion, give or take,' said Roland, 'and if only one in a hundred million supported life of any sort, I'd have to spread myself pretty thinly to cover even those. So many others, like Brian, help me look after 'green' life on their home system's planets. And when I'm not on assignment like now, I roam the star-ways of the galaxy, looking for signs of new life.'

'Why are you bothering with us?' said Oliver. 'We're so insignificant.'

'Because Earth has a very unusual web of *energy paths*,' said Roland, 'which, incidentally, allowed mankind to 'realise' dreams.'

'Myra briefly mentioned dream-reality,' said Oliver.

'Does 'Gaia' mean anything to you?' said Roland.

'Isn't it a new-age belief about the living nature of the planet?' said Oliver.

'It was based on an idea,' said Roland, 'that living organisms interacting with their inorganic surroundings form a self-regulating system, helping maintain conditions for life on the Earth. So, if the world becomes 'out of balance' in some way, there's a natural mechanism to restore it to a stable equilibrium.'

'Are the energy paths involved in the process?' Oliver asked.

'They're crucial to it,' said Roland, 'and, as I've pointed out, as well as providing a balancing mechanism for the planet, they are how human dreams travel towards realisation. They really do possess mysterious power – in the east they were known as 'Dragon Paths,' and in the west many religious sites were built on them.'

'Do I need to know more about them?' said Oliver.

"Yes, it's essential," said Roland, 'even though direct experience of them would be impossible. We'll talk more about them later, but for now I want to work on the more *practical* side of our case.'

'Sounds good,' said Oliver.

'I suggest that you might open our case,' said Roland, 'by describing mankind's achievements. And after that, in view of its poor record regarding others, you'll need to demonstrate its *potential* for benefitting other terrestrial life. And last must come its greatest strength – the creation of *dream-reality* via the portal network, on Earth's Shadow-side.'

'Can we take each in turn?' said Oliver.

'Of course,' said Roland. 'Let's start by supposing you're an alien observing Earth from space. What might lead you to think mankind was the dominant species there?'

'The presence of cities, roads, airports and ships,' said Oliver. 'That's evidence that humanity is better organised on a larger scale and more technically advanced than any other species. And our libraries, museums, churches, even government buildings, would reveal cultural life, unknown elsewhere on the planet.'

'A reasonable point,' Roland said, 'but if 'dominance' is simply a matter of size or biomass, humanity would be well behind krill and bacteria. And long-lived trees cover far more of the planet's land mass than man. As for organisation – insects are much more numerous than humans, and co-operate very effectively. And if adaptability is the criterion, a virus, or even a bacterium, can mutate and adapt much more swiftly than any human.'

'So much depends on your viewpoint!' said Oliver.

'Indeed, and although our case must be based on what you say, it will not be *human* judges at the Inquiry.'

'I'll remember that,' said Oliver, 'but I feel I can still make a strong case for man, even bearing that in mind.'

'You must also build into your case,' said Roland, 'something showing man's capacity for empathy with other species.'

'I'll need examples of good practice,' said Oliver, 'not bland statements of intent, like *addressing* climate change.'

'Widely quoted,' said Roland, 'and universally ignored.'

He then opened a drawer in his desk and took out a manuscript, which he said was written many centuries ago by an Indian sage, describing his experience as a novice monk when his master gave him a mantra to use when he meditated. In common with such practice, he was never to reveal it to another, and he was faithful to the command for many years. But one day he sought out his master, who saw that he was troubled.

'The mantra has given you much wisdom,' he said, 'and you have shared that gift, but you fear its power for good will be lost when you have passed on. Find a way to preserve its benefits, but do not forget my instruction.'

The novice meditated on the problem but found no solution until, one day, he thought of the tree growing outside his window, which had been there for as long as he could remember. He wondered: *might he not speak to it and share the mantra, describing all the thoughts that*

138

stemmed from it, without breaking his word? This he did, and his master told him that this action, following his instinct without disobedience, was the product of right thinking, for there were many ways of preserving truth and wisdom.

So the monk continued on the path, and the tree and he grew old together. And through the relationship he came to learn that all living things are connected, and love can be shared through anything that lives. He felt his tree had its own 'voice' and he listened to it, as the tree did to his. The creatures it harboured had their songs as well and they shared together what was freely offered to all.

The sage wrote: 'The leaves of the tree sang out my thoughts as they moved in the wind, and the birds in the branches flew far and wide, passing them on, as did the insects and everything else that used the tree for shelter or shade. When the tree was cut down, I had no regrets, for all things must pass. But how far and wide my thoughts must have travelled to all who heard the voices of Earth life through that song of the tree and its leaves in the wind.'

Roland finished reading, folded up the manuscript and said, 'That always reminds me of man's *capacity* for living in harmony with those on Earth, even though separated from him by species and lifestyles. You might consider having a similar example of your own up your sleeve.'

'I'll think about it,' said Oliver.

'And now,' said Roland, 'to our most convincing argument.'

'Even though we are wholly out-matched by AI's capabilities?' said Oliver.

'Artificial life is superior to the natural in many ways,' said Roland, 'but such logic-based cultures are commonplace throughout the galaxy. And what a judge will prize above anything will be unusual attributes in a species, *so long as they are likely to be of benefit to others.*'

'Back to dream-realisation!' said Oliver.

'Don't underestimate its importance, Oliver,' said Roland, 'it's *crucial* to our case. And now's a good time for you to learn *how* dream-matter reaches the Shadow-side.'

'Along the energy paths?' said Oliver.

'Correct,' said Roland. 'Think of them as conduits of a gentle but powerful, irresistible force, an 'essence,' gathering up and transporting the dream-impulses, which, after drastic filtering, arrive at a Master Portal, here to be vetted by a Dream-Master, with only a tiny, tiny proportion allowed to transit to the Shadow-side and become a physical reality.'

'So, if it's true, how could that benefit alien cultures?' said Oliver.

'It's vanishingly rare for any race to be able to preserve the best of its culture,' said Roland. 'Societies are typically *transient* phenomena. And through my travels throughout the galaxy, I have seen that the human ability to keep its treasures in a permanent form is widely envied. Access to it in one form or another would be very attractive to the many species that dream. Perhaps it may turn out to be a *transferable* ability, or if not, one that advanced humans could operate on behalf of other species. In the future, if we are in a position to do so, such humans, using a vastly expanded portal network, might transit to worlds light years beyond the solar system, and take their unique '*thought-capture*' abilities with them.'

'*Will* we reach such an advanced state?' said Oliver.

'I don't see why not,' said Roland. 'If we are permitted to maintain our position on Earth, and given a bit of scientific 'help' to speed up evolution, it will happen sooner rather than later.'

'In summary, I should give examples of mankind's greatest achievements,' said Oliver, 'demonstrate our potential to relate to all life on Earth, and showcase our 'dream-capture' abilities with a view to 'exporting' them beneficially elsewhere in the galaxy.'

'That's about it.'

Roland was about to reply when there was a knock on the front door, and when Doris opened it, she found the visitor was Adrian. After inviting him in, she took him to see the others, and left them alone in the study. Roland and Oliver looked up, surprised to see him. No longer behind the bar of the pub, he looked strangely out of place.

'I hope I'm not disturbing you,' he said politely, 'but I heard that Oliver was around, and as I was passing, I thought I'd drop in and welcome you back.'

He walked towards them, and Roland said quietly to Oliver, 'Stay where you are.'

Oliver remained seated, while Roland got up and approached Adrian. After briefly shaking hands, the publican moved towards Oliver, who gestured for him to join him. Adrian sat down on a nearby chair and Roland took his place opposite Oliver.

'What's happened to you?' Adrian said, looking closely at Oliver. 'You look years older with all that white hair. Been getting involved in things you don't understand? Things that are none of your business.'

'Some welcome,' smiled Roland. 'Who told you we were here?'

'You keep out of this, old man,' said Adrian, pointing a finger at him.

'Better get that seen to,' said Roland, looking at Adrian's clumsily bandaged hand, through which blood was seeping.

'And you mind your own business,' said Adrian. 'We've got things to discuss, young Oliver here and me.' He turned away from Roland, hunching his shoulders.

Roland started to get up, and said, 'If I were you, Adrian, I'd think about leaving.'

'It's *him* who should be going,' muttered Adrian, pointing at Oliver and raising his voice, 'carrying on with Molly.'

'You didn't come here to talk about her,' said Roland. 'What do you really want?'

Adrian's face turned red with fury and, breaking out into a heavy sweat, he lifted the heavy bag he'd brought with him and threw it on the desk. He began to undo the clasps, twitching violently as he fumbled with the fastenings.

'Get away, Oliver!' shouted Roland, now on his feet, as Adrian wrenched a large kitchen knife from his bag, and began scything the air with it. Pushing back his chair, he advanced on Oliver, who backed away, holding up an arm to ward off the attack, until he felt he was against the wall.

Adrian shouted triumphantly and moved in, throwing the heavy knife from his left to his right hand, before lunging forward. 'Didn't you know I'm an adept of the black arts?' he screamed, slashing at the arm Oliver had thrown up to protect himself. 'Ha!' he yelled as he struck home and blood gushed from the wound.

Roland leapt forward and, grappling with Adrian as he drew back for another thrust, dashed the knife from his grasp. Oliver sank back, shuddering from the shock, desperately trying to stem the bleeding, and Roland hit Adrian very hard in the stomach. He crashed to the floor.

'Adrian,' Roland said quietly, 'stop this now.'

'Out of my way, old man!' shouted Adrian, struggling to get up.

Roland, looking him full in the face, murmured something and Adrian fell back, writhing on the floor. 'Spawn of Vormint, last vestige of darkness, your time has come,' said Roland, grasping his wrist and twisting it. Every time he squeezed harder, Adrian squirmed and squealed.

'Out you come!' said Roland, and wispy, white vapour poured from Adrian's mouth and nose as he sank down. It writhed and curled away across the floor, turning brown before dissipating.

'Yet another of their little tricks to get at you,' said Roland to Oliver, white-faced and trembling, still desperately trying to stem the blood pouring from his arm. 'Vormint left a residue of himself in Adrian when he transited with you, tiny, but enough to be troublesome. He had made himself so vulnerable, silly fellow, that it was easy for Vormint to manipulate him.'

Adrian slumped onto the sofa before sitting up with a puzzled expression on his face, looking at the bloodied knife in bewilderment. Doris, having heard the noise, hurried into the room. She took one look at Oliver and told him to sit down, while she rushed away for something to staunch the blood. When she returned, Roland turned to her and said, 'I'll get Adrian away from here, and make sure he won't remember a thing. I'll be back soon, and then we'll decide what to do about patching Oliver up properly. So much for his recuperation!'

He then got the dazed Adrian to his feet, bundled him into his car and drove him home, leaving the publican fast asleep on the sofa in the sitting room. When he came back and told Doris about Adrian's attack, she knew that simple physical treatment would not cure him. They both went to the study and found him curled up on the sofa, weeping and exhausted, nursing his injured arm. Doris bent down and cradled his head in her arms, soothing him like a child.

'I can't go on like this,' he said. 'The Eldritch nearly killed me, and now this… what's next? Will it never end?'

'Listen, my dear,' said Doris, 'your wound came from a source which may have inflicted on you more than physical harm, and I will have to treat it in a special way. It will leave no mark, and asleep you will know nothing of what I have done. Trust me when I say it's urgent and essential, and I am able to do it.'

'Yes, you know I'll trust you,' said Oliver. 'Will it hurt?'

'Not a bit,' said Roland, lightly touching his forehead. And then Oliver's mind slipped gently into a quiet darkness that soothed the throbbing pain and quietened the dull fear.

A little later, Doris told Roland that she had removed all traces of poison from Oliver's injury and boosted his metabolism to help him through the trials ahead. And after a night's rest, he should be able to continue on his journey as planned.

***

In the morning at breakfast, Oliver seemed back to normal, and all traces of his injury had disappeared.

'I didn't expect that attack,' said Roland, 'but we can't stop now. Do you need more time to recover?'

'No,' said Oliver, 'we've lost enough through my wanting to be at home. Let's move on.'

'Very well. But before we do,' said Roland, 'I want to make sure you're quite clear about human dreaming and the Shadow-side. Is there anything about it that we haven't yet covered?'

'Yes,' said Oliver, 'I was going to ask about Wayland's Smithy – the place that Myra and I saw on the print in the Speech House.'

'How could I have left that out?' said Roland. 'It's where the Master Portal is located. The dream-matter travels through many conduits and, after being filtered on the way, ends up in the main Dream-path, which flows into the site of the Smithy.'

145

'So that's why we were directed to go to the Speech House,' said Oliver, 'because the site is so critical for the whole process of realising dreams.'

'Yes, and if the opposition wanted to start destroying the Portal network and eventually all access to the Shadow-side,' said Roland, 'it's likely that they would attack the Master Portal first.'

'Who exactly are we fighting against?" said Oliver.

'Ovoid for a start – he's always yearned for AI dominance,' said Roland, 'but until now has kept quiet, waiting for his time to launch an attack on 'natural life.' The advance of AI, leading to the tipping point for dominance, has given him the opportunity he's been waiting for. We think that Malesch, the powerful entity who transited with you, came to help him oppose us. We don't yet know much about him, or where he's come from, but Sebastian's people are trying to find out more.'

'But why go to the Shadow-side when the issue will be decided here on my Earth?' said Oliver.

'Don't forget Ovoid has been over there illegally for many ages,' said Roland, 'and, at first, they will need to confer there. I've no doubt they are so strong they can find a way to transit back here when they wish to mount an attack.'

'Will it come to that?' said Oliver.

'If things aren't working out to their advantage, I think they'll attack the Portal soon, together with its Dream-Master. No doubt they have allies on the Shadow-side as well, who may carry out a similar assault at the same time. And if the portal falls, so does

146

our case. No judge would look kindly on a species that let that happen.'

'And if they succeed, mankind's unique advantage would be lost,' said Oliver.

'Quite so,' said Roland. 'The Shadow-side would lose contact with new ideas and creatures, and its essential vitality would disappear. Devastating.'

'When do you think they'll attack?' said Oliver.

'At any moment.'

'So what can we do?'

'Keep calm. We must use the time we have by giving you first-hand experience of other life-forms on Earth,' said Roland, 'and the wood-wide web, and one of the planet's greatest strengths.'

'I'll do my best,' said Oliver, 'but remember that I've now been burned, beaten and stabbed, and the pain in my feet is getting worse. And now I have a slight headache.'

'Horace can relieve your physical suffering,' said Roland, 'but only you can provide that sense of humour.'

"And on that cheery note…' said Oliver, 'let us laugh our way to victory!'

13

'What do you know about trees?' Roland said to Oliver as they sat on a bench under an oak in a meadow by the river.

'I can recognise most of the common ones,' replied Oliver,

'Any idea about how a tree *functions?*'

'Vague schoolboy memories about transpiration and photosynthesis,' said Oliver.

'You seem to know more than most people,' said Roland. 'And what about *woods?* People feel fond of them without quite knowing why. Are you like that?'

'I've always liked being *in* them, but I can't say I've ever felt deep feelings *for* them,' said Oliver.

'Have you now changed your mind about woods, plants and trees?' said Roland.

'Of course,' said Oliver. 'When the woodland in the Forest of Dean protected me from that dreadful creature, I was standing there afterwards thanking the plants, shrubs and trees for hiding and protecting me, and meaning it with all my heart!'

'Anything else you remember feeling?' said Roland.

'Yes, now you mention it: a strong feeling of 'oneness' with the natural things around me,' said Oliver. 'I'll never feel alone again in a wood. '

"The 'oneness and the whole," said Roland. 'Did it occur to you that helping you was risky for them?'

'Not at the time, I'm afraid,' said Oliver.

'When I suggested that tree life on other worlds might be seen as the dominant species,' Roland continued, 'I wasn't joking. Few humans know how arboreal networks interact with other organisms, or how important they are for life on Earth. As for the trees themselves, hardy, long-lived and patient, they'll abide long after man has gone. And there's great wisdom in old trees, if only man would learn to *listen* to them.'

'But I couldn't possibly *feel* like a tree,' said Oliver, thinking how strange it was that such familiar things, looked at like that, could seem so alien.

'If you'll close your eyes and allow me to touch your temples, we'll go somewhere where you can,' said Roland.

Oliver nodded his agreement, thinking, *Here we go again!* as he felt the same compression he'd experienced before riding on Lance's back.

'You can look around now,' said Roland, after the feeling had ebbed away. 'Don't be afraid, nothing will harm you here.'

Oliver cautiously opened his eyes and saw that they were in a dark tunnel with brown, wrinkled walls, like the shell of a walnut. Above them the roof arched away high into the darkness, and below he sensed dense, humid air, heavy with the deep scents of sap and living wood.

'Where are we?' he breathed.

'In a cell of the cambrium layer of a tree,' said Roland. 'Do you sense anything?'

'A strong, deep beat like an enormous heart, throbbing to the rhythm of an immensely strong pump, sucking up a great weight of liquid.'

'Just imagine the power needed to raise water high into every part of a tree, every branch and every leaf,' said Roland. 'What you're hearing is nothing less than the potent life-force of a healthy, strong and well-nourished tree.'

'What a gigantic hydraulic powerhouse a whole forest must be!' said Oliver.

'Now close your eyes again,' said Roland, 'but prepare yourself.'

Oliver did as he was told, and when he opened his eyes he saw they were in a similar place, but one where the walls were yellow and cracked, and the air thin and dry. Then a high-pitched scream, like a dentist's drill boring into his skull, jolted him upright, and he clenched his fists until the nails tore at his palms.

'We'll go back now to where we started,' shouted Roland through the noise. 'Close your eyes.'

Oliver heard the reassuring sound of water being transported upwards, and saw they had returned to the healthy tree. 'What was that awful sound?' he cried.

'That was a drought-stricken tree crying out for water,' said Roland.

'But trees have no mouths, how could it do that?'

Roland explained that when the flow of water was interrupted, it generated vibrations in tree trunks, similar to human vocal chords responding to the passage of air in the windpipe.

'Are you saying trees scream with pain?'

'Yes, they do, and give signals to warn their neighbours as well.'

'Please, no more trees in torment!' said Oliver.

'It gave me no pleasure to subject you to that,' said Roland, 'but now you'll remember *feeling* the anguish of a living thing suffering in your natural world for want of water. You also felt the sheer power of a healthy tree, pulling water from the ground through its roots and transporting it to the leaves, to evaporate as water vapour into the atmosphere. Taking in the sun's energy, transforming it into new growth, trapping carbon and releasing oxygen into the air. That's how trees live. Any thoughts?'

'Mainly a feeling of guilt that we share this world with these beautiful and wonderful natural treasures,' said Oliver, 'living things who give us so much that we take for granted. But we destroy great swathes of woodland and plant life for short-term advantage or profit. So much waste, and harm to us and the planet. We must see them nurtured and protected from harm.'

'Just keep those emotions fresh in your mind when you're presenting to the Inquiry,' said Roland. 'And now another journey, so close your eyes and hold on.'

Oliver felt the familiar pressure of his light touch on his forehead, and when Roland told him he could, he opened his eyes. But before he could focus on the view, super-heated air, dusty and dry, scorched his throat. When he'd recovered, he looked around, and saw that they were sitting under an acacia tree, surrounded by an arid semi-desert of withered grass, hardy plants and tough, thorny shrubs, all bathed in a shimmering sheet of quivering air.

'Where are we?' he whispered to Roland, sitting beside him.

'Somewhere in the Kalahari Desert, I hope,' he said. 'At least, that's what I specified.'

Oliver knew better than to pursue the topic, and in any case felt far too hot to even think straight.

'We've seen that trees communicate with each other when in pain,' said Roland, 'but that's not all. Keep still and watch.'

The next minute, to Oliver's astonishment, a full-sized giraffe appeared and began to feed on a nearby umbrella thorn acacia. Suddenly it stopped eating and moved on, ignoring adjacent trees, and resumed its feeding a hundred yards away.

'Did you see that?' said Roland. 'As soon as the animal began eating its leaves, the acacia pumped toxic substances into them and the giraffe moved on. Meanwhile, the tree produced a scent warning its close neighbours of the predator, so that they could prepare their own toxic defences. Trees further away were too far for the smell to reach them, and the giraffe moved on to eat their un-poisoned leaves. In the same way, when they were being attacked by insects, the trees attracted beneficial predators to help them and their neighbours.'

'Like humans warning others of danger and helping them,' said Oliver.

'Let's move on,' said Roland. 'Did you know that trees interact through the fungal network around their root tips?'

'I thought all fungus did was attack wood and leave it rotten,' said Oliver.

'Much more than that,' said Roland. 'It's vitally important for the health of the whole Earth. Tree roots extend at least twice as far as the tree's crown and are linked to a dense network of filaments called 'hyphae.' One teaspoon of forest soil can contain many miles of these, and over time, a single fungus can cover many square miles.'

'Can we make contact with a web like that?' said Oliver.

'Yes, indeed, and it's essential that you do. But you'll need a specialist to help you, like your old shrub friend, Brian.'

'But when I last saw him, he was far away on the Shadow-side.'

'Ah, the impossible only takes a little longer than the difficult,' said Roland. 'Why don't we go back to my garden, and see what we find when we get there?'

'Don't tell me,' said Oliver. 'Close my eyes, and whoosh!'

***

They were back under the oak tree with a familiar figure sitting on their bench. Oliver recognised Brian at once, and his heart leapt up as he ran to greet him.

'Hello, my human friend,' said Brian, giving his infectious grin. 'You've got friends in high places! One minute I'm in Arcadia and then, wham, I'm here. And good day to you, Lord Roland.'

'Brian, I've been inside a tree!' shouted Oliver. 'And we've been in Africa!'

'Got some good friends on those plains,' said Brian. 'Good, *thorny* folk there, tough as they come.'

'Hello 'deep sleeper,'' said Roland. 'How's my best and dearest pupil?'

'It's been a long time,' said Brian, as the two embraced.

'Are you ready for another surprise?' Roland said to Oliver, pointing towards a tall, stooping figure coming towards them from the house.

'Remember me, my dear boy?' said the man to Oliver when he reached them.

'Yes, of course, you're the necromancer who made me small enough to ride on Lance's back!' said Oliver. 'And helped me recover from my injuries. It's a great pleasure to meet you again, Sir.'

'The privilege is mine,' said Horace, his eyes twinkling. 'A *'necromancer'* you say, how kind. But in reality, I fear, simply a jobbing peddler of party tricks.'

"But you're far more than that,' Oliver said, smiling at him in pure affection.

'Yes, we all know why Horace Magister is known as the 'Modest,' said Roland, 'and with his help, you and Brian will enter into a sunless world beneath us, undreamt of by men in their blinkered existence in the light above.'

Oh dear, that sounds ominous, thought Oliver. 'What exactly are we going to see?' he said.

'We'll see a fungus's cottony web, which humans called the 'mycelium,'' said Roland, 'and see how its fine network of filaments or hyphae mix with the tree's soft root hairs, extending its capacity to gather nutrients.'

More co-operation between life-forms on Earth, thought Oliver, *totally independent of man, and, as usual, largely unknown by men.*

'The hyphae, unlike some trees that could be competitive with different species, like to *co-operate,*' said Brian, 'but don't think 'selfless generosity,' nature doesn't work like that. And don't think small either. The largest known organism on Earth is a fungus, covering 2000 acres and weighing in at 660 tons.'

'And all under our very noses, or should I say 'feet,'' said Oliver.

'We're going to be smaller than before, and even at that level, you'll feel the harmony of nature,' said Brian. 'Just imagine, Oliver, how few humans, even those with microscopes, have ever seen what you're about to see. And certainly no human has gone where you're going!'

'Just how small will we be?' said Oliver.

'That really does worry you, doesn't it?' laughed Brian.

'I can't help getting nervous,' said Oliver. 'Compared to me you all seem so *adult.* You don't think twice about moving through space and time, appear to have lived for ever and all know one another. It makes me feel so… small and alone.'

Brian shot Roland a quick glance, who said, 'I'm sorry, I keep forgetting about your injuries, and how strange all this must seem to you.'

155

'And I'm only a little human,' said Oliver, close to tears.

'Call your hawk, Lance,' said Horace unexpectedly, 'and we'll leave you together for a little while.' He looked at Brian and Roland and the three of them moved away from the great oak under which they had all been standing.

Oliver, now feeling a little ashamed of his outburst, but still raw and uneasy, wondered how calling the bird would help. But he summoned Lance, who fluttered down onto his outstretched arm.

'Have I failed you in some way?' Lance said, ducking his head and fixing Oliver with his cruel, unblinking yellow eyes. 'Have I ever ignored your summons, or left you unaided or alone in peril?'

'No, no, Lance,' said Oliver, 'you've always come, and you've never let me down, and I wouldn't be here without you.'

'And if you felt yourself in danger," said Lance, '*anywhere,* even in the furthest reaches of your galaxy, and you summoned me, do you think I would not come to you?'

'I suppose not,' said Oliver.

'Well, if there's nothing more,' said Lance, 'I'll be off.'

'Goodbye, Lance,' said Oliver, strangely reassured. He gave a sigh and, looking across to where the others were standing, heads bowed, deep in conversation, waved and said he was ready to go. He watched them slightly nervously as they walked towards him.

'Did that help?' said Horace gently when they reached him. 'I might tell you that no other human known to me has ever been granted the power to summon an Aide of Power, like Lance, avian or otherwise.'

'That's very good to know, and thank you all for your patience,' said Oliver. 'Shall we move on now?'

'Well, if you're sure,' said Roland, 'we'll take up where we left off, and I seem to recall that you were asking about how small you'll need to be to see the mycelium.'

'You must have heard of a 'micron," said Brian. 'Do you know how small it is?'

'Not really.'

'Think of the thickness of a human hair,' said Roland, 'that's about fifty microns across. The little fungal filaments, the hyphae, are about ten on the same scale, so when we descend to view them, we'll be about as tall as a human hair is wide, and the hyphae will be like pipes as high as our knees.'

'But how will we *see* them in the earth?' Oliver protested. 'They're deep down in the soil. And how will we *breathe…*?'

'Don't worry, all that will be taken into account,' said Roland. 'Now, that's enough questions. Over to you, Horace.'

'There's really nothing to alarm you, said the old man kindly. 'I'll summon a special portal, and you'll feel a slight tingling, nothing more.'

Oh yes, thought Oliver, remembering his previous trips and fearing the worst.

***

They were in a dark cavern, surrounded by huge clumps of brown matter, with white tubes running from and between them.

'Now, that wasn't too bad, was it?' said Brian cheerfully.

'I've had a worse trip,' said Oliver. 'It's dark, but I can see quite clearly.'

'Some of the things down here are bioluminescent,' said Brian.

'Those white things like pipes. Are they the hyphae?' said Oliver.

'Yes, intertwined with the roots of the large oak above us.'

'Did I see one of them *move*?' said Oliver.

'Yes, you saw it pulsating,' said Brian. 'Just gently feel the surface of the one in front of you.'

Oliver hesitated before putting out his hand and touching the shiny, white surface of the nearest filaments. It reacted immediately and he jerked his hand away. It felt to him as if a muscle lay beneath the pallid skin, and he looked at it carefully.

'They're very sensitive both to touch and thought vibrations,' said Brian. 'Try it again, but don't be afraid this time.'

Oliver did as he was told, and the surface, gently vibrating, seemed firmer and warmer than before. He felt an impulse moving from his hand to his arm, and an image came to his mind of the hydrae interacting with the delicate roots of the trees above. The picture expanded, until he was almost *feeling* part of the great oak above, and then of the huge forests of trees, all connected, alive and pulsing with Earth energy.

'Do you sense it?' said Brian, softly. 'The oneness and the whole.'

'It's so *energetic* but comforting, too,' said Oliver. 'If only others could see it like that. By the way, is that something moving towards us, over there?'

'There are other... things down here, that don't concern us at the moment,' said Brian, hurriedly.

'Such as?' said Oliver.

'Mites, springtails and weevils – untold billions of them on Earth, thousands everywhere on every scrap of land,' said Brian, 'and it's better we don't meet any of them.' He turned towards the creature and spoke softly, and it backed away and disappeared into the darkness.

'I've noticed that all the hyphae are moving gently,' said Oliver.

'Yes, they operate like fibre-optic cables, using electrical impulses as well as chemical compounds.'

'How fast do the impulses move?'

'Only a third of an inch a second, and that's slow, even by human standards.'

'And nothing like fast enough to transmit all the vibrations of human dreams,' said Oliver.

'Let's not digress,' said Brian. 'Remember you're here to feel mankind's unity with nature. And now we must return to your 'real world' size. I'll summon a portal, and eyes closed again, please.'

***

They were under the oak tree again, normal size, and nothing seemed out of place.

159

'How did you feel about that experience?' Brian asked Oliver.

'Very humbled,' he said. 'My feeling of oneness after touching the filament, and the vision of the whole Earth as one great forest, was breath-taking.'

'At that level you're getting a feeling about nature's unity in a way that very few humans ever have before,' said Brian. 'Bear that in mind for the future.'

Roland then did something rather unexpected. 'Oliver, my dear boy,' he said, 'would you mind if we three had a little chat on our own about your next step? I'll explain more later.'

'Very well,' said Oliver, puzzled, and leaving the others under the oak tree, he walked towards the riverbank, sat down and watched the current slowly moving the water with hardly a ripple.

'What's all the mystery?' said Brian to Roland, when Oliver was out of earshot.

'Oliver's appreciation of the 'oneness and the whole' is working really well, it'll help no end at the Inquiry,' said Roland.

'So, what next?' said Brian.

'I think it's essential that he has first-hand experience of a Dream-path,' said Roland.

'What! That would mean him going far, *far* down,' said Horace.

'You can't be serious,' said Brian. 'Tell him, Horace. No human could stand that miniaturisation or the pressure. I've hardly been as far as that myself, and never alone.'

'It's never been done for a small organism like him,' said Horace, 'even to get him down there would be at

160

the very limits of my powers, let alone his. And there's always the problem of re-entry. The timing would need to be flawless.'

'Not to mention his fate at the deepest level if it goes wrong,' said Brian. 'No, it's just not on, even his hawk couldn't reach him there.'

'I suppose a carefully *phased* re-entry would be feasible,' said Horace, pulling at his beard, 'worth a paragraph or two in the Necromancer News!'

'And he'd be dead, poor lad,' said Brian, 'and fond of him as I am, it's getting late to find a new candidate.'

'Lord Sebastian would certainly not give his blessing to such a risky business,' said Horace, thoughtfully.

'You mean he'd go bloody ballistic,' said Brian, 'and I for one don't fancy living out my aeons in some ancient galaxy, with all the lights going out, thank you very much!'

'Would he need to know?' murmured Horace, inspecting some foreign matter that had emerged, blinking, from his beard.

'Perhaps not,' said Roland. 'Even so, only fair on the boy to know this would be no walk in the park. It wouldn't be like being down with the hyphae.'

'But look at what we'd gain,' said Roland. 'His credibility at the Inquiry would be enhanced out of all recognition.'

'Perhaps we might put it to him,' said Brian, 'sound him out. But I'll only agree if we make it plain to him why he's going, and something about what to expect down there. And I insist on being with him every step of the way.'

'Brian, is that wise?' said Horace. 'You're much more valuable to the universe than the little human chap. Of whom I'm also fond, I might say.'

'Those would be my conditions,' said Brian, 'take them or leave them.'

'Perhaps I might take further *advice* on the matter,' said Horace. 'A peer related *symposium* might be a judicious option, or even a less structured *sounding out* of informed opinion…'

'That's 'no' then, from Horace,' said Brian. 'What about you, Roland?'

'The gains would outweigh the risk,' said Roland briskly, 'we'll drum up another sage. Thanks for your time, Horace.'

'I didn't say I wouldn't do it,' said Horace, hastily.

'Really?' said Brian. 'Anyhow, let's put it to Oliver.'

Roland went over to him standing by the stream and asked him to join them under the oak.

'We've been discussing your next move, Oliver,' he said, when they were all together, 'and we'd like to sound you out on our proposal.'

'Oh yes,' said Oliver, an uncomfortable feeling creeping over him.

'We think that now you're ready to see the Dream-path along which the pulses move.'

'I'm not really authorised to get you down that far,' said Horace, 'and I'd have to use a very, *very* special part of the portal system, but at present, I can't see any harm in doing it.'

'How much further down?' said Oliver.

'Have you heard of the 'Planck limit'?'

'Physics isn't my strong point. Sounds small from what you say.'

'Ten to the minus twenty of the diameter of a proton', said Brian. 'Doesn't mean much to you, does it?'

'Not a thing.'

'It's so unimaginably tiny that I'll try to describe it. Suppose the whole Earth was a huge ball made of solid steel, and a fly lands on its surface every hundred years and then takes off immediately. Just imagine how long it would take for the ball to be reduced to nothing by the friction generated by the fly. That is the time in years you would need to get down to the Planck level in a spaceship travelling at a thousand miles an hour.'

'So why are you telling me this?'

'Just above the Planck level lies a mysterious realm, unknown to your science, where the Dream-paths function. Even so far down in scale it's still a region *of* the human world, sharing its physical laws, and not deeper still, where ordinary physical laws break down.'

'And running through these Dream-paths is an *essence*,' said Horace.

'I heard about that,' said Oliver. 'But what exactly is it, and what does it do?'

'It's a moving force,' said Horace, 'attracting the vibrations emanating from human dreams, like flies to a flypaper.'

'So it's a *current* whisking them along to the Master Portal,' said Oliver.

'Yes,' said Brian, 'and although it acts like a fluid, it actually looks more like a filmy mist.'

'What's important,' said Roland, 'is that we all feel that, if you experienced it yourself, it would greatly benefit your standing and confidence when presenting at the Inquiry.'

'You want me to go down to the *Planck* level?'

'Yes,' said Brian, 'but don't worry – I'd come as well, and always be with you. And all you'll have to do is take a deep breath and *feel* the force for yourself. Think how thrilling it would be to see the Dream-impulse, in their slippery bubbles, all clumping together, and then follow them through to where a few contenders emerge at the Master Portal.'

'Brian, you have done this before?'

'Old hand at it, Brian,' said Roland, 'and he'd hardly take you somewhere he didn't know was safe. And Horace wouldn't sanction something *dangerous,* now, would he?'

'But once we're down there, how will he know where we are?'

'You can be sure he's got that in hand,' said Brian. 'Don't worry, he'll be employing advanced hermetic skills. Wonderful, *technical* stuff, which we wouldn't understand. And he'll give us plenty of time down there.'

'Will we meet the Dream-masters?'

'Not unless they want us to,' said Brian.

'But we still have to warn you that this is a little… irregular,' added Horace, 'and if Lord Sebastian knew what we're proposing, he might have the *slightest* of reservations.'

'But what fun…!' said Brian.

'Well, if you're all *quite* sure it's safe,' said Oliver…
'and if it's going to be *fun* for Brian, what's stopping us!'

'Nothing,' said Horace. 'Let's proceed.' He then
recited some words and summoned a faint filmy portal
entrance out of thin air, and the last impression Oliver
had of him, from inside when the door was closing, was
the reassuring smile behind his white beard. But what
he didn't see was that behind his back he had crossed
the fingers of his left hand, and was holding tightly on
to his good luck rabbit's foot in the other.

14

Oliver felt that he and Brian were cascading down and down, spinning and twisting, through dusks with gold-rimmed clouds, and mornings radiant with blinding dawns. To where time held no sway. But after an age, or the blink of an eye, the portal slowed and then stopped. And Oliver, astonished to see that the walls were now wafer thin, peered through the veil and saw that they were in a place of eerie gloom.

Then, far away, like a tiny distant rising sun, he glimpsed a point of light and strained his eyes to see it clearly. Suddenly it burst into incandescence and, like a moth to a flame, he left the portal and went hurtling towards it, plunging through an immense black tunnel. He saw dazzling impulses racing beside him as he flew, fierce flashes of intense light fusing and then fizzing out in bursts of dazzling energy. Then he was plummeting further and faster inside a blinding duct, weightless as light, with metallic fireflies dancing around him and sparkling filaments of light appearing and then vanishing with the faintest of flickers.

After shedding the portal like a redundant carapace, Brian kept pace with him with his human shape, filmy and fluctuating, displaying a rainbow of colours like the skin of a cuttlefish. And then glowing particles, like sponges of pure energy, began attaching themselves to his body in glittering clumps, like white cells in human blood engulfing an alien invader. And as he became more and more of a glistening ball, his flight faltered, and Oliver, forging ahead and looking back, saw a look of panic on his face as it vanished. But just before he disappeared from view, the golden envelope enveloping him flew apart, and an object like a slim, green organic bullet with trailing legs broke free, surged past Oliver and spiralled along the tunnel, gathering speed as it went. Brian, if it was still him, dived into a side passage leading off the main tunnel and disappeared.

Oliver, aghast, glanced down at his own body, and was reassured to see that he retained the outline of a human shape, although a more transparent one than on the earth above. Being human and perverse, he was too enraptured to be afraid, whirling as he was now through a shining mist, his body sparkling with energy. He noticed he was surrounded by vibrating particles, snaking through the silvery light, leaving quivering wakes before dissolving into bursts of powdered light. And below he saw glittering silver trails, like the wake left by a pod of playful dolphins aquaplaning on a watery sheet of shining mercury. It was far beyond his powers of description, beggaring any image that man had conceived or created.

And then, to his relief, Brian was back in his old, unshackled shape and matching his headlong speed.

'What happened?' shouted Oliver, recalling that human speech consisted of *vibrations,* like so much else around him.

'Something here means to harm us,' Brian shouted back. 'It tried to ingest me, but I have the power to escape that, but you must be careful!'

What an incredible universe it is! thought Oliver, awed by the beauty of this realm, so far beneath the mundane world of Man. And the universe above looked from images to be as achingly lovely as this-and as unreachable.

'We're far enough down to see the Dream-spheres,' shouted Brian, pointing ahead. 'See them linked in a line to form sequences.' Oliver saw the taut, shining globes, like a row of large party balloons bobbing and bumping along, fastened to each other to form a line.

'Each sphere holds billions of Dream-impulses,' shouted Brian, 'and new ones join them all the time, absorbed through their skin. It's a type of osmosis.'

Oliver cried out, 'Can I touch one? I'd like to see what it feels like!'

'Don't even go near them!' shouted Brian. 'We don't belong here! We'll be attacked as foreign bodies if we're not careful. Just watch and learn!'

Oliver was silent, content to be wafted along, even at what would be breakneck speed on the earth above, but his reverie was cut short by a cry from Brian.

'Beware! There's danger ahead!' he shouted, but his voice was drowned out by what sounded like the noise of rushing, turbulent water. Oliver saw they were approaching a tributary joining the main sequence, and the essence, that subtle but powerful current carrying them along at great speed, seemed to be slowing down here. He soon saw the reason why.

'There's a huge, spidery thing blocking the channel!' he shouted. 'And it's diverting the spheres away from our Dream-path.'

'It's a Dream-monitor,' shouted Brian, 'the first stage of getting rid of unwanted Dream-matter. It's highly sensitive to unwanted and toxic impulses. The spheres are forced against it by the essence and squeezed, releasing beads of 'good' dreams that go through its mesh to continue their passage in the main stream. See them clustering together to make new 'clean' spheres further downstream. The vast majority are diverted into the side channel. So now you know how most of the Dream-matter is rejected before it gets near the Master Portal. Would you like to get a closer look at a monitor?'

'If I must!' shouted Oliver

Brian began moving his arms to get into a position where he could help him get nearer the mighty membrane, without being swept into the middle of the stream, where its current was strongest. 'Follow me,' he shouted across to Oliver, but Oliver was caught up in the swirling essence.

'Help!' he shouted, grasping at a sphere, which at his touch lost its lustre, turned brown and became wrinkled.

'Leave it alone!' bellowed Brian. 'It's toxic!'

Oliver let go but, still enmeshed in a jostling mob of Dream-sequences, hurtled towards the great creature – if it was one – spanning the stream in front of him, its monstrous outstretched legs connected by a tough, yellowish net-like membrane. Surging towards it, he saw the spheres being compressed to extract the 'good' Dream-matter and then being jetted away into the tributary by the force of the essence expelled from the membrane's 'mouth', like the funnel of a colossal squid.

Brian, paddling frantically, rammed him hard into the narrow slip of current flashing past the monitor and through into the main current of the essence, which sped them on at great speed until they found a sheltered part of the stream where they were able to take stock.

Now that they had paused from their headlong flight, Oliver was fascinated watching the antics of creatures around them. Transparent fish-like creatures with fiery-tipped tentacles shimmered past them, slim-bodied essence-snakes chased spinning worms with their mouthparts gaping wide, and scorpion-like shapes scuttled and danced in moving circles. And others, dim and shadowy at first, became luminescent for an instant before flashing out of existence in a burst of light.

'Can they really be *alive* down here?' he shouted across to Brian.

'Why not?' replied Brian. 'Things live in your deep oceans. But don't let these creatures divert us from our main purpose here.'

'Sorry,' said Oliver. 'Perhaps we can see what happens to the rejected spheres after they've been diverted by the monitors? You said it was a natural process. Wouldn't the Inquiry want me to know about that?'

'I was about to suggest that,' said Brian. 'It's an essential part of the process linking the Dream-world and the green realm. There may be a slight problem, however.'

'What is that?' said Oliver.

'How to get *back* to this main stream,' said Brian. 'Did you see any *empty* tributaries on our travels?'

'You've not done this before, have you?' said Oliver, after a moment's thought.

'And, as we were saying,' said Brian, ignoring the comment, 'we don't know how long we've got down here at this size.'

'I said that would be a problem,' said Oliver.

That annoyed Brian and his body colour became kaleidoscopic. 'Horace allowed us enough time to complete the whole journey to Wayland's Smithy,' he snapped, 'and he mentioned *gradual size acclimatisation.* But never mind, we'll take the next junction, the very next,' he shouted, 'and don't blame me if we're never seen again!'

'Thank you so much,' said Oliver meekly. 'Sorry.'

Brian grinned, and his skin regained its normal healthy hue. 'Get ready, there's a junction coming up,' he shouted as they swept towards a tributary, allowing the surge generated by the Dream-monitor's maw to push them into the slower, smaller stream.

'Where do you think this tributary will take us?' Oliver said.

'No idea, but the Dream-sequences don't seem worried,' said Brian, 'so why not see what happens? Look around and learn – that's why we're here, isn't it?'

'It's getting darker,' said Oliver, 'we're definitely slowing down, and everything here looks *muddy.*' It was

171

hard to get rid of the idea that they were sailing along on the surface of a liquid, with the rejected spheres bobbing along beside them.

'Any life here?' said Brian.

'All kinds of things,' said Oliver, staring around him. 'Some are like rays with flat bodies and big suckers. They seem aggressive.'

'They're guarding something,' said Brian, 'but what? Feeding grounds? Or are they scouts for a large predator? Don't annoy them, if they sense us as a threat we may be in big trouble.'

'Too late,' said Oliver, for as he spoke, creatures were rising up around them, several of the pliable ones wrapping themselves around Brian's legs. He shook them off violently, but their companions kept pace with them from a distance.

'We've been spotted by something!' Oliver shouted suddenly. 'It's shadowing us, and its *huge*.'

'Where is it?' Brian said quietly, moving quickly towards him.

Oliver pointed to where a large shape, only slightly denser than the essence, was hovering below them, so big that it appeared almost suspended in the current.

'Hold out your arms, and grab hold of my hand,' said Brian, 'and then spread-eagle yourself. We must look as big as possible.'

Oliver did as he was told, and the shadow, as if bored, slowly peeled away and disappeared. 'That didn't find us by accident,' said Brian. 'We are taking big risks being here. Just remember what you're seeing.'

Something dramatic was now happening as their tributary split into smaller streams with the lines of Dream-sequences following different routes.

'Must we follow them?' Oliver shouted to Brian, pointing to the Dream-sequences.

'It's how you'll see what happens to the discarded Dream-matter,' Brian shouted, 'and then you'll really appreciate how *natural* processes on Earth relate to Dream-realisation on the Shadow-side.'

'Will any side passage do?' shouted Oliver.

'Sure, let's take the next one,' said Brian.

It was not difficult to follow the spheres along the tributary as it left the main channel, and as they followed the current Oliver noticed the essence getting denser, almost *organic*. And was it his imagination or was the atmosphere becoming clammy and close?

'There were so many of these side channels,' said Oliver, 'siphoning off Dream-sequences from the main stream, and it's almost as if there are *banks* on either side, like being in a river.'

'It should remind you of Roland's world of living filaments,' said Brian, 'but, of course, we're still vastly smaller than anything on upper-Earth. And remember it's your last chance to be down here, so try and relate what you see to the task in hand. And bear in mind that I don't always see the same as you, young human! We'll compare what we see later.'

Now the essence was sweeping them towards a dark, narrow opening in the channel, like a tunnel. But before going on, they steered themselves to one side of the stream and paused to get their bearings.

'Can you hear a sound like running water up ahead?' Oliver shouted. 'That meant turbulence in the main channel, and it's so dark inside the tunnel I'm a bit worried about what we'll find there.'

'Don't be,' said Brian, cheerfully. 'Whatever's going to happen to the Dream-spheres, they don't seem worried, so why should you?'

'I don't see how that follows,' said Oliver.

'Time for your famous sense of humour,' laughed Brian and Oliver gave him a shaky grin.

Keeping closely together, they nudged their way into the main stream, following the spheres sweeping along towards the tunnel's entrance. As they passed into the dark, Oliver noticed with alarm strong, twisting tendrils hanging down around the rim of the tunnel's mouth. The roof above them was now becoming very low and something brushed his face, which he hoped was harmless cobwebs. What light there was came from the spheres, moving beside them, gently glowing at first and then becoming suffused with golden light. Then, as the tunnel continued they began butting into each other, like giant hippos in a river fighting for dominance. These violent collisions resulted in the smaller ones becoming ingested into the larger ones, creating bloated, monstrous globes, with taut, blotched skins stretching almost to breaking point and changing colour from golden to copper, ending up an organic brown. Discarded skins fell away from the couplings and, although wrinkled and palsied, were eagerly snapped up by a host of obscene crab-like parasites scuttling below.

Oliver watched in disbelief and wonder until, quite suddenly, he felt heavier and the outlines of the world around him became sharper. And then he felt the first pang of piercing regret that his time here was coming to an end, and he was no longer a traveller in a glittering world where fantasy and fact danced as partners so beautifully together. And lurking in his mind was the thought that this realm and Shadow-side were every bit as 'authentic' as human 'reality', only more lovely and a lot more *interesting*!

And then they were out of the tunnel, into an open, dimly-lit space, with the great bloated spheres beside them.

'Everything seems to be getting bigger', Oliver said, feeling like Alice in Wonderland taking a sip from the 'Drink me' bottle.

'Yes, we're leaving the sub-atomic world behind', said Brian.

'And far, far away, judging from your image of the depth of the Planck limit', said Oliver, looking about anxiously, although nothing dramatic seemed to be happening. *How is it that they can change relative to their environment and not notice its effect?* he wondered.

'And we didn't feel a thing!' said Brian. 'Horace's gradual size acclimatisation actually worked!'

'Just look at the expanded spheres!' gasped Oliver, watching what was happening to the vast bloated globes, wrinkled and flabby, some with angry boils on their palsied skin, containing untold trillions of Dream-impulses. For he was witnessing one of the most extraordinary sights anywhere in the galaxy – the absorption of the discarded

Dream-matter from the spheres through the hyphae into the wood-wide web.

Oliver pointed at the huge bubbles nuzzling into the bank and rubbing themselves vigorously against the dozens of rootlets protruding from its surface.

'Yes,' said Brian, following his gesture, 'minute tendrils from the mycelium attach themselves to the spheres' skins, and burrow through to absorb the Dream-matter inside. It's the start of a miraculous process, ridding the essence of the Dream-toxins through the root system to the trees above, which transpire and vent them into the atmosphere.'

'And nothing is wasted,' said Oliver, thinking of the spheres' unwanted skins being eaten now by a different type of crabs from the ones in the tunnel. 'Are they really so noxious?' he said. 'We think of sweet dreams, don't we?'

'I think we're about to get an answer,' Brian said, grimacing, as a boil on the palsied skin of a nearby sphere exploded, releasing a puff of fine particles. As the cloud of Dream-dust floated over him, Oliver felt a revulsion deeper than any disgust he'd ever experienced.

'All those repressed ideas and ugly thoughts humans can't express in the day are there by the billion,' said Brian, 'and some impulses are so rotten and noxious they spread poison to the rest. That's why we must keep well away.'

'So humans generate toxic dreams, and fungi, roots, and trees have to clean it all up,' said Oliver.

'Something like that,' said Brian, 'and the Dream-paths cover the whole planet. Nothing like it exists anywhere in the galaxy, and it *must* be preserved by Man for the planet's sake. And that's what you must impress on the Inquiry – how this wonderful Earth operates in tandem with that other miracle: Dream-realisation.'

'Which no artificial organism can infiltrate or copy,' said Oliver. 'If Roland's responsible for green processes like this, on millions of planets, he must wield great power.'

'Perhaps too much,' said Brian.

'What do you mean?' said Oliver. 'Isn't he a close friend of ours?'

'Has a history of extremism, old Roland,' said Brian. 'Fanatically green, of course, as you'd expect. And, between us, not keen on human dominance on your Earth.'

'Can you blame him?' said Oliver. 'His green systems have to clean up human mental waste, while we destroy his forests for gain, ruin productive land, displace natural habitats and leave rubbish everywhere.'

'Agreed, and you must persuade the Inquiry that Man has the *potential* to change,' said Brian, 'for there are signs that things are slowly improving. And even though it's too little, too late, I believe that compromise between humans and nature is always the best solution in the end. But that is not Roland's view. Remember he was reluctantly drafted in to help your bid.'

They continued to glide on their way, feeling their bodies grow ever bulkier as the lightness of their beings faded. And at last, from the gloomy realm of root and hyphae, they entered a dim cave where a great number of essence tributaries met to compose the main Dream-path. And there the purified stream of essence, carrying the now-precious Dream-matter, went underground to the Master Portal, only rising again to face the final scrutiny of the Dream-Master at the Smithy.

Where, if it was supremely fortunate, a tiny, tiny amount would end up realised on Shadow-side, helping preserve the very best of Man. Separating and protecting the sublime from the mundane. And also removing the gross imaginings of so many members of the 'dominant' species inhabiting the bleak, grey world that gave them birth.

15

'Journey's end!' Brian said to Oliver, after they'd adjusted to the 'upper' world in the cave. 'How do you feel having seen things no human has ever witnessed before?'

'Privileged, and a bit daunted,' said Oliver, 'but much more confident about the Inquiry. I'm ashamed I ever doubted any of you for a moment.'

'Think no more of it, my dear fellow,' Brian said, brushing away the remark with a modest cough, more relieved about his safe return than Oliver would ever know.

'What now?' said Oliver.

'I'll first spy out the land,' said Brian, pointing out through the narrow cave opening to a rutted track following the contours of the undulating downland before disappearing beyond the brow of the hill away to their left. 'Open country like this always makes me nervous, especially near a busy part of the Ridgeway like this.'

'The path's very special around here, isn't it?' said Oliver.

'Particularly now,' said Brian, 'because, as we know, the essence runs underground from this cave and along a major Dream-path beneath the Ridgeway to the Master Portal in Wayland's Smithy. I don't know why the portal creators, whoever they were, chose to put it here. Probably because there's an unusually powerful force here, even for an energy path.'

'And those men who built the Smithy to bury their dead here must surely have felt that too,' said Oliver. 'And the Ridgeway was always a very important and ancient route.'

'Old by human standards,' said Brian, 'but, of course, only the blink of an eye to whoever created the portal. Or mine, for that matter. It's a continuation of the Icknield Way – the whole path runs from south Norfolk to the sea in Dorset. And certain parts, like this, have been considered sacred for many ages.'

'Even Myra, who didn't know Earth well, felt its spiritual power when she saw the print of Wayland's Smithy in the Speech House,' said Oliver. 'But I guess I'm the first human to *know* about the portal and the Dream-path here.'

'Certainly,' said Brian, 'but sensitive humans over the centuries have felt its power, and folklore spoke of it passing 'out of the known and into the mystic, leading to kingdoms of great danger and reward.'"

'You seem to know a lot about it,' said Oliver.

'Yes, but that's enough for the present,' said Brian. 'We really must get on.'

He moved towards the cave's entrance, but then paused and looked closely at the weathered chalk path winding around the curve of the hill. He held up his hand to restrain Oliver from moving, and said, 'Keep very still, something's wrong.' He left the cave and began walking slowly towards the Ridgeway, and then stopped. Looking back, he beckoned Oliver to join him.

'I can't see anything,' said Oliver, squinting in the bright sunlight.

'I'm still getting a strong feeling that something here's not right,' said Brian, looking around, 'and it's strange to see the sky as empty as this. There are always birds using the up-draughts here. Always.'

'Where exactly *is* the Smithy?' said Oliver.

'It's behind the flank of that hill,' murmured Brian, pointing, and then put a finger to his lips.

'What should we do?' said Oliver.

'Whatever's here is near the Smithy,' said Brian, 'and I must find out what, but without being spotted.'

'Lead on,' said Oliver, 'you know the country round here better than me.'

'We're west of the burial mound here,' said Brian, 'and, as I said, here it's hidden from our view by that incline on our left. I suggest we work our way around it, so that we can reach Odstone Coombes, which will give us a good vantage point over the site. Remember the name. We may need to meet there again.'

Keeping a low profile, they crept along the ridge of the small escarpment until Brian gestured to Oliver to stop. He then crawled forward and cautiously peered over the brow of the low hill. 'As I thought,' he said softly, and waved to Oliver to come and join him. From their position Oliver could see over the landscape of undulating downland, along which ran the track of the Ridgeway. Halfway along its length it was punctuated by a small ring of beeches and shrubs, in the middle of which was a stone burial mound, its dark entrance flanked by four large standing stones.

'That's the Smithy,' said Brian, pointing to the structure, 'with the Ridgeway path running closely beside it.'

Oliver looked at the site of the Master Portal, and the armed soldiers around its perimeter, with more troops straddling the path. Red and white plastic strips attached to yellow cone-like uprights had been strung across the track like an official barrier, with others circling the upright stones of the burial mound. And away to his left, further up along the Ridgeway path, he could see a large brown army tent, with even more armed guards on duty. It was clear that the valley was filled with soldiers, either in groups or on sentry duty, and they were all carrying arms.

'Don't move, and don't make a sound,' said Brian quietly. He pointed to the tall figures, perfectly still and silent, as if waiting for something. 'What do you make of them?'

'They're very disciplined,' said Oliver, 'standing as steady as rocks! What are they, and what are they *doing* here?'

'I suspect they're *androids,* robots who look like humans, and they're here because of you,' said Brian. 'Probably programmed to prevent you using the portal to get back to the Shadow-side. As you know, they can't follow you there.'

'But how did they know we'd be here?' Oliver stuttered.

'Good question, my friend,' said Brian, grimly, 'and I'll bet Roland knows something about it.'

'*Roland!* Surely not!' cried Oliver.

'You don't know this, but we planned to transport you to the Shadow-side as soon as we'd come from the essence stream,' said Brian. 'It would be far safer for you there. We knew they'd step up their attacks now that you're becoming more valuable with the Inquiry getting nearer.'

'But Roland wasn't the only one who knew you planned that!'

'But he's the only one who's been coming under huge pressure from the green side about your bid,' said Brian.

'What kind of pressure?'

'The Natural lobbies in a number of rocky planets in the galaxy have been going through a very rough time recently,' said Brian, 'and losing out to Artificial intelligences in a number of key sectors.'

'You make it sound like the lead-up to an election.'

'It's something like that, for the green power base as a whole depends on the support it gets from Stellar Federations,' said Brian. 'Does that make it seem even more like one of your political campaigns?'

'Sadly familiar,' said Oliver, 'but…'

'Not now, Oliver,' said Brian, 'we've more pressing things to do than worry about galactic politics. And to get things moving, I'm going to go down to the Ridgeway and see if I can find out more about those troops down there.'

'They'll spot you immediately!'

'Not like this,' said Brian with a grin, waving his hand and transforming himself into a walker, complete with worn anorak, sturdy, dirty boots, and a bulging backpack. He completed the package with a wild beard and the demeanour of unquenchable enthusiasm about rights of way that all dedicated ramblers seem to possess from birth.

Brian backed away from the ridge and when he was out of sight of those below, stood up and strode away. Oliver watched him, heart in mouth, as he saw him, having retraced their steps, walking along the Ridgeway towards the manned barrier. When he reached it he smiled and waved his hand.

'Are you blind or merely stupid?' said the soldier nearest to him. He was tall with piercing blue eyes, a symmetrical smooth face, and was wearing a perfectly blank expression.

'I'm neither, nor am I an offensive lout like you,' said Brian. 'This is a right of way, and I'm entitled to use it. So get out of my way.'

"We're not going anywhere,' said the soldier without moving a facial muscle, 'and nor are you.'

'What the hell are you doing here, anyway?' said Brian.

'Listen, mate,' said another identical soldier, this time a sergeant, judging from the stripes on his sleeves, 'dangerous old land mines farther along the track, left over from the war. And we've got orders. Can't let you through, it's in your own interest. Sorry, mate.'

Brian waved his arms and gave a look of disgust at the soldiers, who regarded him with blank indifference, before turning away and walking back the way he'd come.

When he re-joined Oliver he said, 'They are androids, as I thought, but not many humans would spot that. The trooper was programmed to be rude, and the other to say there are old land mines in the valley left over from the last war.'

'Where have they come from?' said Oliver.

'They're likely to be clones, with slight variations, of a single fighter that Ovoid has managed to transport from a part of the Shadow-side which you haven't seen,' said Brian. 'Where there's a big War Studies School. But he'll have needed help to get it over. No prizes for who helped him do that!'

'If it's true, let's hope that's all Roland did,' said Oliver.

'I must get word to Lord Sebastian and tell him what's going on,' said Brian.

'Do you know where he is?' said Oliver.

'*One* of him has been more or less permanently on the Shadow-side,' said Brian, cryptically, 'and I want to see him face to face.'

Oliver thought for a moment, and then said, 'But you can't use the Master Portal to transit with those soldiers there, can you?'

'Oliver, I'm going to let you into a great secret,' said Brian, 'but only because I'm going to have to leave you for a while, and your life's in grave danger.'

'What?' said Oliver, with a sinking heart.

'Even Lord Sebastian doesn't know this,' whispered Brian, 'nor does Roland, and he *must not* find out what I'm about to tell you.'

'Go on,' Oliver breathed.

'Wayland's Smithy's an elaborate *decoy,*' said Brian. 'There's a portal there, but it isn't the *Master Portal*, and there's no Dream-Master here.'

'Why doesn't Lord Sebastian know where it is?'

'He doesn't need portals to get around the galaxy and, in the past, he's not given them much thought,' said Brian. 'Now he's recognised their importance to the Shadow-side, and knows that Ovoid, helped by Malesch, plans to destroy them.'

'What do you want me to do now?' said Oliver.

'Keep hidden – I'll show you where to lie low and you must keep very still. Things are coming to a head. And if Sebastian agrees it's the only way of getting you safely to the Inquiry, it may mean a physical encounter between his forces and Ovoid's supporters.

'What are you going to do now?' said Oliver.

'I'll tell Pan that I want to meet Lord Sebastian, and am planning to transit through the 'real' Master Portal,' said Brian. 'It's not far from here, but it's better you don't know where. If I'm prevented from doing that, I'll arrange to get word to you about what to do next.'

'Is there more?' asked Oliver.

'While I'm away try to *quieten* your thoughts,' said Brian, 'and, if you can, avoid trees and woodland plants. It's unlikely, but Roland may have put the word around the green realm, and told them to reveal your presence to the enemy. Now I'll take you to where you can hide and rest, and stay there until I get back.'

Beckoning Oliver to follow him he crept along behind some bushes and pointed to a hollow where he could lie hidden. 'It's safer for you if you are asleep, for then your thoughts are less revealing,' he said, touching Oliver softly on his temple, who curled up and immediately fell asleep. And darkness descended on the downland, which had seen many past encounters but few as crucial as the one about to take place on the morrow.

***

It was getting light outside when Oliver was awoken in the sheltered hollow. With his heart in his mouth he sat up, and looking around to see what had disturbed him, saw a face peering through the bushes hiding him from view.

'What do you want?' he gasped.

'From Lord Sebastian, I bringing you word,' said the man, who had tightly curled hair and a bronzed, chiselled face.

'Who are you?' cried Oliver.

'Son of Hermes,' said the man, patting his chest, 'famous God.'

'Really?' said Oliver, looking closely at him.

The man handed him a sealed note and said, 'Am like divinity of antiquity. Please to read note, and…'

'Yes, *yes*,' said Oliver, looking at Sebastian's seal on the folded parchment before opening it. He read: 'Hermes's boy is carrying this message to you because he's fast and reliable. He's also expensive and tricky. Check if he's got real wings on his ankles, but be discreet, he's touchy about things like that.'

Oliver took a deep breath and said, 'Please don't take offence, but would you mind showing me your feet?'

'Is great outrage!' said the man.

'Don't think for one moment,' said Oliver, 'that I'd ask a divinity like you for something it wasn't vital for me to know.'

'Alright then, innit,' said the messenger, taking off his shoes and colourful socks, and showing two small wings sprouting above each ankle. 'Good, eh?' he said. 'Toes and wings wiggle same time. Also have big...'

'Yes, very nice,' said Oliver hastily. 'What's your name?'

'Big name, Hermaphroditos, short name Hermos,' he said. 'Short better. Pleasing now to read message.'

Oliver scanned the letter which said Sebastian feared that Ovoid was out to kill him on real Earth, and was trying to immobilise the Master Portal before destroying it completely. He'd put up a powerful force-field blocking the entrance, which Sebastian's people were working to remove. Conflict between them was inevitable and imminent, and he was concerned about getting Oliver safely onto the Shadow-side. He ended by saying that the messenger would answer any questions he needed to ask, and that Oliver could assume it was him speaking.

Oliver looked at Hermes junior, who was sitting down looking rather petulant.

'Ambrosia you got about the place, has you?' he muttered.

'Does that seem likely!' said Oliver.

'Me just asking,' said Hermos.

'Can we be serious?' said Oliver. 'I've important questions to ask Lord Sebastian.'

The god slumped forward, and when he looked up, his eyes were glazed, and he spoke with Sebastian's voice.

'Be brief, Oliver, this connection's difficult. Pricey, too.'

'Is there going to be an actual *physical* fight?'

'Yes, at your level,' said Sebastian. 'On the higher planes, more of a *spiritual* encounter.'

'When's it all going to happen?' said Oliver.

'Probably tomorrow at Wayland's Smithy.'

'Why so soon?'

'Events have unfolded very rapidly,' continued Sebastian, 'Roland was compromised by Ovoid, who sensed his lack of warmth for the human bid and kidnapped Doris, forcing him to reveal information about our plans.'

'So that's why we found the soldiers standing outside the entrance to the Smithy,' said Oliver, 'waiting for us to emerge from the Dream-path.'

'Yes,' said Sebastian, 'they were there to prevent you using the portal to get to the Shadow-side, if Ovoid hadn't yet blocked it with his force-field.'

'Did Brian manage to get through to you?' asked Oliver.

'When he tried to get to me, he was attacked by Artificial militia, who left him for dead,' said Sebastian, 'but he'd just enough strength left to use the other portal to transit, and tell me to contact you.'

'A dear friend lost,' said Oliver, bitterly, 'and all because of Roland's treachery. How *could* he betray us so badly?'

'That's not entirely true,' said Sebastian. 'Ovoid released Doris when he understood that Roland wouldn't help them any more.'

'What forces will you be facing?' said Oliver.

'I'm taking advice on that,' said Sebastian. 'Localised conflicts like these involve numbers limited by Cosmic Decree. But I anticipate meeting our arch-enemies Ovoid and Malesch, almost certainly supported by elementals, like the ones you have already encountered, and also the militia located at Wayland's Smithy.'

'And who's on our side?' said Oliver.

'You know them already,' said Sebastian, 'but perhaps not as you'll see them ready for battle.'

'What can I do to help?'

'Be ready to transit to the Shadow-side as soon as you can,' said Sebastian, 'and in extremis, utter the words I gave you when we first met. We'll meet later at the Smithy. Goodbye, for now.'

'Wake up, Hermos, son of Hermes,' said Oliver, 'you're free to go now. Thank you so much.'

'I was pleasured to help, mister human,' said the messenger. He twitched his toga and disappeared into thin air.

And now all there was for Oliver to do was keep under cover, be quiet and hold his nerve. It hadn't seemed much to ask at first, he thought, but as darkness fell and with nothing to do, trying to stem his anxiety about the battle to come was the most difficult thing he'd done on the whole journey.

But at least he could review what he'd seen and done. And feel, in spite of everything, that he was now ready and able to produce for the Inquiry his very best shot.

16

Wayland's Smithy, the ancient Neolithic burial mound next to the Ridgeway, is over five thousand years old and still generates a profound sense of unease in many visitors, even to this day. But few can have viewed its surroundings with more apprehension than Oliver, awakening in his hollow sleeping place with the rising sun lightening the sky and a light dawn breeze wafting over the downs.

It had taken a few moments for him to remember where he was and why he was there, and when he did his heart began racing at the thought of what lay ahead. He longed to stretch his legs on the springy turf and breathe in the fresh air of the awakening downs, but he knew he must lie low and keep hidden.

Then it occurred to him that, without revealing his location, he could use Lance to find out if anything was happening, And when he called the falcon, without further ado, he appeared and fluttered down onto his outstretched arm.

'Do you need my help, Master?' he said, looking down at him with his hard-yellow eyes, and then jerking away his head, with its cruel beak, in the manner of his kind.

Oliver could never get used to the deference shown to him by the great hawk. It never failed to astonish him that this merciless, beautiful killing machine, with its deep, inherent wildness, addressed and treated him with such subservience, obeying him instantly, without question.

'Do you know when Lord Sebastian will appear?' Oliver said.

'I understand he will be here at any moment now, Master,' said Lance, 'and you'll see him coming over Dragon Hill.' He flicked his head to indicate where he meant, and Oliver nodded, for he knew the location, further north along the scarp from where he'd been hidden. The 'Dragon,' of course, referred to the figure of the famous White Horse of Uffington carved in the shoulder of the hill.

'Will he be alone?' he asked.

'Probably not,' said Lance, 'as his allies may now have joined him from other planes, or distant parts of the galaxy.'

'They'd better hurry,' said Oliver, 'time's getting very short.'

'Time is not a problem in capable hands,' said Lance. 'As well as being permitted to flow, it may be *adjusted* should the need arise.'

He's getting very literate, thought Oliver, *or do I mean articulate?*

'Either or both would do,' said Lance.

'Please go now, and let me know when he's arrived,' said Oliver, puzzled but too pre-occupied to question his response.

'As you wish,' said Lance, surging up and away, leaving Oliver wondering about his words. He returned shortly, perched on his outstretched arm and nodded towards the north. 'They have come, Master,' he said, 'and if you agree, I'll join them when the time comes to add my weight to the fight.'

'Of course, all shoulders to the wheel,' said Oliver, wondering if 'wings to the lift-off,' would sound better to an avian.

'Not really,' said Lance.

Oliver bit his tongue and, holding his hand to shield his eyes from the morning glare, looked towards Dragon Hill. At first all he could see was the close-cropped, undulating downland, with the breeze ruffling the short grass, and then something moved above the brow of the hill, and he saw figures emerging out of the morning haze.

Leading the way came Pan, striding along, using a robust human form, sturdy and strong; less battered and more regal than Oliver remembered. After him came Meg and Myra, walking and laughing as they approached, tall and relaxed, lithe and confident, deeply bound together in their shared sisterhood. *But how few they are!* thought Oliver, his heart dropping. How could they face the terrible power of Ovoid and the evil Malesch, the awful elementals and the heavily armed android soldiers? *Roland and Brian, you should be here with us now*, he thought with a catch in his throat.

But one person, the most important, was missing. Oliver scanned the slope and then there he was, Lord

Sebastian, bringing up the rear, wearing a benign smile, dressed in Norfolk brown plus-fours, like a gentleman in an Edwardian shooting party, looking urbane and elegant. And with him was a great dog with shining coat and bright, intelligent eyes.

'Master, I think you might safely emerge to welcome them,' said Lance.

Oliver stood up and ran towards the hill, laughing with pleasure to see them, relieved that they were all there.

'Well met, my dear Oliver,' said Lord Sebastian, smiling and holding out his hand as the others parted to let him come forward. Then the sisters embraced him, and Pierre leapt forward with a soft bark of pleasure. Oliver wrapped his arms around the great dog.

'Forgive me asking,' said Oliver to Sebastian, 'but have you brought any *reinforcements*?'

'You think we are so few?' laughed Sebastian, and turning, pointed at a forlorn figure following them at a distance. 'Don't forget our rear-guard,' he said, 'consumed with misery for siding with the enemy.' Roland looked up at the sound of his name, and quickened his pace to join them.

'Let me help you, my Lord!' he cried. 'You can't fight them with so few. Even Brian has gone.'

'Oh, come here and join us,' shouted Sebastian over his shoulder in mock despair, 'you rascal, you know we need you.'

Roland stared at him in joy and wonder, and ran forward, tears streaming from his eyes. Wringing Sebastian's hand, he cried out, 'My Lord, you can rely on me! To the end! To the end!'

'Well, not the bitter end, I trust,' said Sebastian. 'And time now to recruit another fighter. Come here, Pierre.'

At first the dog backed away and growled, but then came forward and licked his outstretched hand. Then, with the fur standing up on his back, he gave a mighty shake as if emerging from water. A dense cloud enveloped him, and when it cleared, the figure of a tall, bearded, blonde and blue-eyed man stood in front of Lord Sebastian.

'Dramatic as always, Asada!' said Sebastian, smiling as they embraced.

'The joy of release, brother,' said the man, 'even though I have resided in this fine animal, who will have been unharmed in his hosting.' He held out his hand to Pierre, and fondly stroked his head. 'Go to your master,' he said, nodding at Oliver, 'and serve him as well as you have me.'

'This is Lord Asada, my brother,' said Sebastian, 'and a Guardian of the Galaxy, dedicated to maintaining cosmic order.'

'What he means,' laughed Asada, 'is that we work discreetly, anticipating difficulties before solutions become too drastic. In the case of the coming crisis on Earth, I have used the bodies of two splendid Earth animals – Pierre here, and our late friend Cain.'

'Thank you, Asada,' said Sebastian, 'and now let me explain what lies ahead.'

And so two Lords of the Galaxy, a restored Galactic Director, two advanced spirits of space and time, an ancient woodland deity, a human with a literate falcon and a great dog sat down to discuss the coming conflict.

'What we must do,' Sebastian began, 'is gain time while my people weaken Ovoid's block on the portal enough for Oliver to slip through. He can then prepare for the Inquiry on the Shadow-side.'

'With so many soldiers guarding all the approaches to the Master Portal?' said Roland. Oliver was on the point of saying it wasn't the real one when he recalled he was sworn to secrecy.

'I have now received the 'rules of engagement' from…elsewhere,' said Sebastian, 'and the opinion is that we are fairly matched.' This, to his slight annoyance, was greeted with a burst of laughter.

'No doubt our superior abilities in strategic *planning* have helped our betters ignore the disparity in our numbers,' he said sternly, quelling the levity with an icy glance.

'Who exactly are we facing?' said Pan.

'Basically three sorts of opponents,' said Sebastian, 'each of whom we'll need to meet with different tactics.'

'The armed androids would be one,' said Pan.

'Correct,' said Sebastian, 'and our first concern.'

'They will be clones,' said Myra, 'and I suppose Malesch's evil little helper Vormint is among them.'

'Even if he's not,' said Sebastian, 'it is these troops we must first engage.'

'We don't even know how they're armed,' said Meg.

'Or how many there are,' said Roland.

'Or which of us you want to take them on,' said Myra.

'I'll return to who we'll deploy against them in a moment,' said Sebastian, 'but let's turn, for a moment, to the next foes – the 'elementals'. Ovoid has been allowed three, and we know they can be powerful, certainly much more so than the foot soldiers.'

'The ones I met were very different,' said Oliver. 'I suppose they come in all shapes and sizes.'

'Yes, they are unique creatures,' said Roland, 'designed for specific purposes, using material to hand that can vary.'

'Those facing us will have been designed for aggression,' said Meg. 'It's difficult to anticipate what they'll be like.'

'I'm looking to you to deal with them, dear sisters,' said Sebastian. 'Their weakness lies in their molecular structure, for they are rapidly assembled from local matter. I'm sure focussed energy will carry the day with them.'

'We'll be delighted to take them on, my Lord,' said Meg. 'I've a score to settle with their sort.'

'So, that leaves Ovoid and Malesch,' said Oliver.

'Asada and I will meet them on a more *rarefied* plane, whose nature only we can understand,' said Sebastian. 'We don't know the limits of Malesch's powers or even where he draws them from, and a confrontation with him and Ovoid could escalate, making demands on us all.'

'Will we ever see you again, if things don't go quite to plan?' said Oliver.

'Never fear,' smiled Lord Sebastian, 'I will return.'

'In some form or another,' Asada laughed.

'Finally,' said Sebastian, 'I have placed an exclusion ring around this entire site, and from now on, no human will be aware of anything happening here.'

'I assume the barriers the androids have been maintaining will also be invisible to humans,' said Oliver.

'Correct,' said Sebastian, 'and now I've outlined the nature of our enemies, let's get down to *tactics*. To get Oliver through the portal we must deal with the androids guarding the portal entrance, but that alone will not allow Oliver to transit, for it's Malesch's *personal* power obstructing the portal. But that will be rectified when Lord Asada and I tackle him on the higher planes.'

'But even the androids will be hard to defeat,' said Roland. 'I'm sure they're a strong force, well-armed and deadly as fighters.'

'You're right,' said Sebastian, 'and I don't want the sisters mixed up in that, for they will need to harness their strength in tackling the elementals.'

'So that leaves Pan and me,' said Roland.

'Not to mention me, a dog and a hawk,' said Oliver. 'Ample reserves, surely, my Lord?'

'While you all have been frittering away your time,' Sebastian said, ignoring the comment, 'I have studied in detail, all the important battles fought on planet Earth over the last four millennia.'

'Have we *time* for this, brother?' said Asada.

Yes, get on with it, thought Oliver.

'The terrain we have before us is similar to the one at the Battle of The Little Big Horn in 1876,' said Sebastian, 'and we are disadvantaged, in many ways, like the Indians at that encounter. But they won. So, like them, we'll disguise our numbers, move swiftly, keep the enemy forces divided, and deliver a decisive blow by *focussing* ou*r* attack. Thereby prevailing over numerous, heavily armed professionals with lightning reflexes.'

'What can possibly go wrong?' said Oliver.

'If you are unfamiliar with undulating downland like this,' Sebastian continued, 'co-ordinating large bodies of troops is difficult, but it favours mobile *irregular* forces who use *guerrilla* tactics.'

'So you want us to rush up and down valleys armed with bows and arrows,' said Roland.

'No, but I have arranged to deploy cavalry troopers who know what they're doing, and what is needed here,' said Sebastian.

'Troops?' said Oliver. 'I don't see any.'

'I think you'll find the answer coming across to meet us,' said Sebastian, pointing at the track leading to their position, and with some heavy breathing and hoof stamping, Wrach, the great Centaur appeared.

'Mornin' all,' he said, a little out of breath, looking fiercely around the gathering containing his former wife and sister-in-law.

'We spoke,' said Sebastian, 'and you have what you need for the heavy lifting.'

'Yes, my Lord,' said Wrach, hefting a mighty stone club, 'all present and correct.'

'They all know it's not going to be easy. There will be deaths.'

'A *chosen* way to go, my Lord.'

'Good, too, for those who make it through the day.'

'Yes, and for them I'm lookin' to you to make good on your promise, my Lord.'

'Glory and honour await you.'

'And ambrosia,' said Wrach, wheeling away.

'Wrach,' said another voice.

'What do you want?'

'Be careful,' said Meg, 'and good luck to you all.'

'Hmmmph,' he said over his shoulder as he galloped away, greatly pleased.

***

This encounter is the only instance in warfare on Earth where two 'phantom' forces met in battle. The centaurs were brought over from Shadow-side by Sebastian using his black hole pass. Like other Shadow folk who transited, they had physical bodies on real Earth that they could use.

The androids were cloned from a single fighting unit also on Shadow-side, which, disguised as a house-bot, 'slip-streamed' with Roland through a portal to Earth. Malesch, who had returned to real Earth using an unknown route, had supervised the cloning of the android in the army marquee on Ridgeway spotted by Oliver. His clones were capable of physical combat on real Earth, and could therefore oppose the centaurs on equal material terms.

***

Because of the undulating terrain, much of the fighting in the first part of the battle was hard to follow. It opened with a strong force of centaurs attacking the main android positions by charging hard from the north, surprising the soldiers manning the Ridgeway south-west of Dragon Hill where it ran near the iron-age fort at Uffington. The speed and ferocity of the attack took the enemy by surprise, although their reaction was phenomenally fast, effective, orderly and disciplined. Even so, before they could deploy properly, many were mown down by the great beasts or battered by their heavy clubs. And after sweeping through their ranks, giving them no time to form defensive lines, the centaurs, turning at the gallop, poured a volley of devastating arrows into their midst. But it was by no means one-sided, and although the centaur leaders now knew that their foes were not immune to heavy physical punishment, a score of their brothers would never see the green fields of Arcadia again.

The plan was now for the force to sweep round in a great anticlockwise movement to meet more battalions from the south, who were charged with destroying the tented area where clones were being manufactured. That force, after crossing the Ridgeway and turning west, would then join the first force to support them in an attack on the heavily defended Smithy.

It worked as planned, and with the tented area, its defenders and facilities destroyed, the two separate units from the north and south met on the Ridgeway and pressed home a ferocious attack. But word had reached the defenders, and the response was immediate and deadly. Before long the battle for Otstone Coombes was nearing a climax, with dead, dying and wounded centaurs littering the ground amongst the splintered and smashed body parts of androids. And although at least the capacity of the Artificials to replicate on the battlefield had been lost, the element of surprise, and the early advantage of cavalry, was draining away.

The heavy fighting was taking its toll on the strength and morale of the centaurs, and the initial impact of their pincer movement faltered and began to fail. Although recklessly brave, they were meeting implacable, relentless opponents, using lasers and heavily armoured. That would be enough to dismay the greatest of human troops in the worst battle ever fought, and those watching could see the frantic wheeling and counter-charging of the centaurs, and the steady ranks of the androids swiftly reforming and pouring withering fire into their ranks.

'Time to withdraw?' said Pan, gnawing at his lip.

'Wait a little, I think,' said Sebastian calmly. He kept glancing to the west but Oliver neither saw nor heard anything to allay his terrible anxiety. And then, after what seemed to him an eternity of waiting, above the sound of the fight he heard a distant drumming, echoing louder and louder through the downs, as a fresh horde of mounted warriors thundered round the brow of the scarp into the Ridgeway, the springy turf scarcely muting the heavy beating of their hooves. This was the weightiest of the heavy cavalry, and with them came Wrach, leading four great centaur clans, fourscore great fighters in each, bearing down on the tomb along the Ridgeway to the west.

The Artificial militia, still excelling in formation and physical prowess, formed a perfect defensive line. But at the last moment the centaurs split into two, and in a vital instant caught their opponents unawares, as both of their mounted flanks turned inwards to join their brothers already fighting fiercely.

The androids' reaction was stunningly fast, and their lasers took out the leading ranks of both charges, but they were already engaged with the first two waves of centaurs from different directions. Now the fresh charge, close-packed rank upon rank of huge, angry beasts, proved irresistible, over-whelming the now heavily outnumbered infantry, who were smashed to pieces by their deafening assault, to lie dismembered and immobile beside the dead and wounded centaurs.

Reining themselves in from the initial assault, the entire centaur force now went berserk, bellowing and whooping, battering their remaining opponents with clubs and axes, mowing down by the score the few still standing, metal and plastic man-sized ninepins falling to their blows, and lying crushed, splintered and broken. Not one android remained operational after the centaurs at last wiped the sweat from their brows and rested their great clubs. Now was the time for remorse for the fallen centaurs, but none to spare for the androids, for whom it would have been quite unnecessary.

Battered and wounded, Wrach waved to Sebastian and the others to come across to the Smithy, and they walked past the scattered remnants of the militia and stood silently surveying the scene of carnage around the front of the entrance.

Wrach flicked his tail and looked defiantly at Sebastian, who was gazing calmly around him. 'Tell me this sacrifice will be worth it,' he said, waving a mighty hand around the site of the battle, littered with the debris of destruction.

'My dear Wrach, all hail to you and your mighty companions,' said Sebastian, adopting his favourite war leader's demeanour, 'valiants in the full vigour of life, bonded by blood and kin, forever joined in our hearts with the fallen, who even now look down from lofty Valhalla, to whose halls they impart an unmatched lustre. This deed will be long remembered in your feasts.'

'And not forgotten by those privileged to have witnessed it, either,' said Asada.

'Husband, it was well done,' said Meg.

'Great rewards await you all in Arcadia,' said Sebastian, 'succour for you and your wounded, and undying respect for your dead.'

'And ambrosia?' said Wrach, a little dazed at the lavish feast of words laid out before him.

'As much as you want, for as long as you wish,' said Sebastian, 'but sadly we cannot come with you to enjoy your just rewards. And now back to your well-earned delights in Arcadia, with our profound thanks.' He waved his hands and the centaurs were all gone, the living and the wounded and the dead.

***

'And now,' said Sebastian, 'we'll take our stand here, by the Smithy. Meg, please put an extra protective ring around the site. Oliver, close your eyes.'

There was a blinding flash and a noise like a thunder-clap, and when Oliver looked again, he saw that the whole of the burial site was enclosed in a shining hemisphere which, fading like the skin of a newly dead fish, wavered for an instant and then vanished from view.

'The next attack will be from the elementals,' said Sebastian, 'and we will give them a glimpse of what they will meet. So now is the time to present ourselves in a more *revealing* way to any who may be observing us. More formal attire, everyone, please.'

At his words, each of his companions seemed to grow, all of them radiated light, and Oliver, astonished at the display, saw that it varied from individual to individual. Meg's figure was clothed in purest white, almost dazzling, while Myra's outward lustre was a mixture of tawny hues, moving and deceptive. Green-tinted beams shot from Pan's steel-leaved chain-mail, flickering and flashing, blinding the eye; while Roland's thick brown tunic with its belt of obsidian was surmounted with heavy, rock-tinted, grey robes. Lord Sebastian radiated power from within a long flowing purple robe, with a belt of silver, and a necklace of dark blue stones shining with a deep inward light. Lord Asada, light blue-robed and now helmeted, carried a staff of iron, whose clubbed head flickered and sparked with energy.

Oliver dropped to his knees in the face of such beauty and power.

'It is only one aspect of reality you see before you,' said Meg, kindly, seeing his confusion and distress.

Things exist that are as far beyond our understanding and powers, as we are beyond yours.'

'I don't want to return to my dreary little world after seeing all this,' Oliver said.

'Always remember,' said Lord Sebastian gently, 'that you are only conscious for part of your human lives, unaware of the treasure that lies in your dreams. And if all goes well, they will be your galactic salvation and the future of your race.'

As he spoke, the air around them shivered and Meg's force-field bulged inwards, as if subjected to an intolerable pressure. The big players were moving into battle, and Ovoid was stirring.

'Couldn't I just *try* to go through the portal?' pleaded Oliver. 'So you can withdraw, and not have to face what's coming.'

'It would be of no use, for Ovoid's force still binds the entrance,' said Myra, 'and he's the *real* source of its strength. Ovoid and Malesch are beyond our powers and, I'm afraid, that's something Lord Sebastian and his brother will have to resolve.'

'*Afraid!*' said Oliver. 'Beings as powerful as you?'

'Of course not,' Myra smiled, 'that's simply a human emotion. As for 'powerful', it's true that Meg and I can transverse space, and sometimes *bend* time a little. But in doing so we might be carrying out the will of others, we do not know; but the lack of an answer will not deflect us from the path we are following here today.'

Oliver opened his mouth to speak but his thoughts were interrupted by a huge booming pulse, which he felt rather than heard. The force-field around them billowed and buckled madly, like a mighty sail bellied out by a sudden blast of wind. It held, but only just.

'Soon the elementals will be inside the field,' said Lord Sebastian, 'and I will leave you in the safe hands of Meg and Myra. Lord Asada and I must away to attend to business elsewhere. Are you ready, brother? Stern foes await us, and we must be steadfast.'

'Oh, yes,' laughed Asada, giving the victory sign in response to his brother's grandiloquence.

'Ready, my dear sisters?' said Sebastian, looking hard and lovingly at them.

'And willing, my Lord,' Meg smiled. And when Sebastian and Asada had gone, the sisters, now alone, began to grow in stature, their forms glittering with light. Oliver, for the first time, felt the full pulse of their power like a physical blow. It was not a moment too soon, for the two elementals had breached the ring of power, tearing a great rent in its wall, their huge wreathing coils of yellow vapour pouring over the threshhold and morphing into huge, dense, familiar elephantine shapes that dwarfed even the sisters. Rigid with fear, Oliver was rooted to the spot as his hated adversaries lurched towards them.

Not so the sisters, who braced themselves and stood their ground. The first elemental lunged at Meg, who recoiled under the blow. The creature moved forward and then struck again, with a projection like a great coiled fist that would have shattered an elephant's skull. Swinging away from her, it then caught the unprepared Myra a mighty blow, with all its weight behind it. Her light dimmed, and she staggered back, almost losing her balance, while Meg leapt forward to steady her, holding up an arm to protect them both from the brute force of another attack. At this, the second creature, sensing their weakness, began advancing on the sisters, who, clutching each other, seeming to shrink in size as their light ebbed.

Oliver, watching in fascinated horror, longed for Sebastian to appear, but help came from another quarter as Roland, armed with only an oaken shield and short sword, interposed himself between the sisters and their foes. Both elementals, as if in surprise, reared up above him, but he seemed to grow to outmatch even them and, as Oliver watched in amazement, took the form of a mighty oak tree. And sheltered for a moment by that shape, the sisters were able to regroup, and their light returned.

Pan, roaring with rage, ran to join Roland, who had resumed his normal shape and size. Together they faced the great creatures rearing up, and proved too agile for the cumbersome beasts, for when one of them struck out, the mighty limb met nothing but thin air. But at one point Pan lost his balance and fell heavily, holding up an arm to protect himself. Two hammer blows that would have felled an ox rained down on his back as he knelt to rise, and he fell forward under the weight of the assault. One of the elementals raised both huge arms above its head to finish him off, and Roland sprang forward, shield upraised, a jet of green energy shooting from his sword, protecting Pan as he struggled to rise.

The turning point of the engagement came when two huge bolts of lightning from each sister hit the monster, which, distracted by surprise and pain, paused and looked around for a second, before launching another attack on Pan. But he'd struggled away, out of reach, and Roland had followed suit, and now another bolt of energy, this time from Myra, struck the other elemental.

Oliver could see that the struggle was resolving itself, with the sisters moving so quickly that they could harry the clumsy monsters with bolts of energy, while Pan and Roland were inflicting severe wounds, jabbing again and again. This began disrupting the molecular structure of the elementals, the loose arrangement of hastily assembled atoms of which they were composed. The discharges were literally causing them to fall apart. And Pan and Roland could now disengage and watch, as great chunks of material, flayed from the elementals' bodies by the laser-like stabs of the girls, flew into the air, dissolving into a fine mist. And as the sisters, with Pan and Roland joining them, grew stronger and brighter, the entities shrank in size and power.

At last Meg looked at her sister and, holding hands, they began whirling together, faster and faster, partners in a diabolical dance of death. It was as if around them spun a great Catherine wheel, sparkling with beautiful but lethal energy, as they moved towards the elementals, slicing through their remaining substance. The elementals made one supreme effort to reassemble, but it was too late, and the monstrous creatures, losing all control of their unreconstructed form, became oily, yellow vapour, which the sisters swept away with their whirling wind.

'It was well done, Pan and Roland,' said Meg. 'Without you we would not have won the day.'

'It was an honour to help,' said Roland.

'Shall we join Oliver, who has been watching the fight?' said Myra, and the four of them walked over to where the others were standing.

'Well done, ladies,' said Oliver to the sisters. 'Remind me not to pick a quarrel with you! Now what?'

'We wait for our Lords,' said Pan.

'How long will they be?'

'Ten minutes, two earth years, a millennium,' said Meg. 'Not too long, I hope.'

'Don't tease him', said Myra. 'Oliver, we'll tell you as soon as we hear anything.'

'It's agonising waiting like this,' said Oliver, 'not knowing what they're facing up there.'

'Difficult for us all,' said Roland.

'I hope they hurry up,' said Pan quickly, 'there's something big and nasty coming our way.'

'It's gone very dark,' said Oliver. 'Is it another elemental?'

'Similar, but much more toxic, stronger than the others, and growing,' said Roland, 'as if it's *feeding* on something,'

'I'll refresh the ring of power,' said Meg.

'Lord Sebastian said there were *three* elementals, and Ovoid might be holding back his reserve,' said Roland, 'but what is it?'

'Whatever it is, it's stronger than the other two combined,' cried Myra, 'and getting more powerful.'

'Huge vibrations,' shouted Roland. 'It's a fear-vampire, the fastest growing thing in the galaxy.'

'The barrier to the portal,' shouted Meg, 'I can feel it weakening. Sebastian and Asada must be winning!

Oliver, get ready to transit while we try to hold that thing back for just a minute!'

Now the creature had reached the re-set shield and was leaning its weight upon the elastic film. It buckled under the pressure, and then the dreadful shape retreated, drew itself up and prepared to charge.

'Oliver, *fear* vibrations drive and nourish it,' cried Myra. 'It's tasted yours, and is ravenous for more. Think of some absurd scene, then *concentrate* on it! Picture it in your mind as long as you can. The portal is nearly open.'

Oliver looked wildly around. The protective envelope flattened and flopped around in the still air, and then the creature broke through. Roland, deathly pale but blazing with zeal, leapt to strike it with his flashing sword, delaying it for an instant as the others ran towards the portal at the Smithy's entrance. It was opening slowly, so slowly, still partially blocked by an opaque film.

'Think, think! The sillier the better!' shouted Pan, his green colour glowing with energy as he ran back to help Roland, still flailing wildly at the monstrous shape. 'Anything will do!'

'A mad tea-party,' Oliver screamed, and instantly in front of him, in Lewis Carroll's own words, appeared, '…a table set out under a tree… and the March Hare and the Hatter were having tea at it: a Dormouse was sitting between them, fast asleep.'

Oliver stared at the tableau before him, his mouth open. The characters, life-sized and real, looked at him with curiosity. Everything was silent for a split second, for his diverted attention puzzled the fear-vampire, and it paused as it was about to crush Roland.

'What does a dentist say to a portal?' the Mad Hatter asked Oliver, frowning.

'What?' said Oliver incredulously.

'Answer the question' screamed Meg, 'the barrier's dissolving!'

Oliver understood, and racked his brains. 'Open wide!' he cried.

'And the magic words, the magic words!' screamed the March Hare.

'Humpty dumpty!' Oliver cried.

There was a huge crack, a blast like a hurricane swept across the space where they were standing, and the great black shape of the fear-vampire, grown enormous now, straddled the shattered shield. Roland and Pan were the first to get the shock-wave and down they went in a threshing of legs, Meg and Myra were pushed to one side and Lance shot skywards. But Oliver and Pierre stood firm.

'The portal!' screamed Meg. 'Go through, you two, go through!"

'Jump, man, jump,' roared Pan, struggling to his feet, trying to stop something from reaching him. Oliver began to run towards the now opening portal, but felt a tug and then a pull holding him back. The film in front of the entrance was wavering now and becoming more opaque as Ovoid's barrier regained its strength. Oliver glanced over his shoulder and saw an appendage from the fear-vampire had snaked out and caught his arm, keeping him back. Lance dropped from the sky, with his cruel beak and claws, straight at the limb. Brian hacked at it with his sword, and Roland gave it a great blow with his shield. Its hold loosened for an instant, and in a flurry of feathers Oliver was through with Pierre beside him. And the portal door closed after them and they were safe on the Shadow-side at last.

17

After their last frantic effort to escape, Oliver lay trembling on the floor of the portal, with Pierre beside him calmly licking a wounded paw. After a moment Oliver felt they were moving, and he turned and thanked the dog for his help.

'Thank those we left behind,' said Pierre, 'like our old friend, Cain.'

'It makes me feel so *unworthy*,' said Oliver.

'Stop feeling sorry for yourself and get on with things,' said Pierre. 'Imagine how I feel without Asada. But I'm an animal, and we have to carry on.'

They fell silent, and when the transit was over and the door opened, they breathed in the pure air suffusing a pleasant meadow on Shadow-side. And while Pierre went off to explore, Oliver, exhausted, lay down and began dozing on the warm, sweet-smelling grass. Suddenly he was jerked awake by a familiar voice.

'All safe and sound?' asked Wedros, smiling down at him. 'And in good shape for the big day.'

'What… what are *you* doing here?' Oliver gasped, looking up at the huge beast.

'Working,' said Wedros.

'At what?' said Oliver.

'I'm the Dream-Master of the Shadow-side.'

'Seriously?' said Oliver. 'When we met you'd just 'done time' orbiting the earth.'

'That 'me' was a clone,' said Wedros, 'all part of Sebastian's clever deception – that way I could vet you, and keep this job under wraps. We're near Wayland's Smithy, by the way.'

'But the Master Portal isn't here,' Oliver said.

'Actually it is,' said Wedros, 'but it was important you thought it wasn't. The opposition could read your mind, like your falcon does, irritatingly discreet fowl!'

'I'm astonished you're a Dream-Master,' Oliver stammered.

'You mean I'm not someone more dignified,' said Wedros, 'with an authoritative bearing?'

'Well, yes, no offence intended.'

'Others thought like you,' said Wedros, 'and look who they recruited. Two went dream-crazy, one 'fell' into raw dream sewage and went mad, and another ended up dream-stalking the authors of 'adult' dreams. Another haunted dream-paths, and ended up mangled in a membrane.

'How did you cope?'

'As you can see,' said Wedros, 'I'm very physically exciting and beautiful, but I'm also coarse, unrefined and vulgar. And that seems to de-sensitise me.'

'But you're the ultimate 'quality control' for dreams – selecting only the very best for Shadow-side.'

'My counterpart on the real side does the quality control bit,' Wedros smiled. 'Between us, Shadow-side's not what it was. For a start, it's full to bursting, with not much good stuff coming through. And there's bad behaviour from some already there. My job's more like chucking out time outside a pub. You don't think I carry this heavy club around for fun, do you?'

'What do you do to them?' said Oliver.

'When I get word they're due for the chop,' said Wedros, 'I ask them to de-materialise. And if they don't... I do it for them,' he said, grinning and hefting his weapon. 'Had that Caravaggio the other day.'

'Who's your counterpart on the real side?' said Oliver.

'No more, now,' said Wedros, 'I've already said too much.'

'Did you see the battle at the Smithy?' said Oliver, changing tack.

'Most of it,' said Wedros.

'You weren't involved?'

'I'm a *Dream-Master*,' said Wedros, 'I've no business putting myself in danger. Anyhow, it was a limited-numbers engagement.'

'But your parents were involved,' said Oliver.

'I was going to intervene if things got tricky, but Brian and I weren't needed.'

'I thought he was dead,' said Oliver.

'Only injured,' said Wedros. 'You were given the *impression* that he died, so others could pick that up from your thoughts.'

'What happened after we made it through the portal?'

'After you left, the fear vampire ran out of fuel,' said Wedros, 'and they polished it off in no time. Then they cleared up the place, for all I know had a cup of tea with the Mad Hatter, and then pushed off. Where to I don't know.'

'What happened on the higher planes?' said Oliver.

'From what I gather,' said Wedros, 'Ovoid and Malesch were getting the worst of it, and ascended to a really high spiritual plane, unlike our boys. Bad news for the bad guys, and now Ovoid's running some dismal proto-galaxy on the far reaches, and Maleschis in 'past rehab,' in a black hole a few billion years ago. A really nasty one, I hope.'

'What about Sebastian and his brother?'

'Sebby's a bit shaken,' Wedros said, 'although he won't admit to it. And Asada's on a primitive planet in Orion, where he's living in a host creature like a cross between an aardvark and an elephant. Happy as a harpie.'

'What now?' said Oliver, feeling rather out of things.

'It's back into the portal with you, and home to meet up with your people and the Chilvers, and wait for the brown envelope.'

'What envelope?'

'The one about you attending the Inquiry,' said Wedros. 'Do keep your eye on the ball, Oliver!'

'I'll keep that advice in mind, next time I'm attacked by a Wendigo!' said Oliver.

'I heard about that,' said Wedros, 'and I thought *that's another one gone,* and they're quite rare. They really need to be protected.'

'Tell that to their mangled prey!' said Oliver.

'The great English humour!' Wedros laughed. 'The gift that goes on giggling!'

'What's in the envelope?' said Oliver.

'There's a form to fill in. If you ask him, Roland will help you fill it in.'

'Can we trust him?'

'Absolutely!' said Wedros. 'He never defected *seriously.* When they saw that the little they'd got from him was all they were getting, they released Doris.'

'Did they harm her?'

'No, but *boy*, was she annoyed,' laughed Wedros. 'She was iced up on one of Saturn's rings, and she hates the cold.'

'How long before the Inquiry?' said Oliver.

'They've cleared a backlog of cases,' said Wedros, 'so it'll be only three Earth days, after they get the form back. And that's meant a change of plan – you've got to go back to the real side.'

'And after all the fuss to get me over here!' said Oliver.

'Sorry, but you'll have to take it up with old Sebby,' said Wedros. 'Take Pierre with you and use my private portal. But don't let on, because you're not authorised to know about it.'

'Ready, Pierre?' said Oliver. 'Let's just *go.*'

'I was just *wondering*,' said Pierre, 'if you might go on without me, and I'll meet you later.'

"Manners maketh dog," laughed Wedros. 'I'm sure the lady will be delighted, you rascal. Don't worry, Oliver, I'll get him back to you soon, never fear.'

'*Toujours la politesse,*' sniffed Pierre.

Oliver wished him well, sent his regards to his friend, and stepped into the gleaming portal Wedros had summoned. He whispered and 'whoosh,' off he went.

***

As soon as the door opened, Oliver stepped outside and the portal was whisked away. He found he was near to the tomb where they had left, and looking around he saw that the cemetery was unchanged and that it was early evening. He picked his way through the decaying memorials in the empty graveyard and took the path by the river leading to his house. *How long have I been gone?* he wondered, and then with a sudden shock, *What if Frank, Cynthia and Molly are elderly or even dead?*

Reaching his house, he paused before walking up the garden path and peering in through the kitchen window. Seeing nobody there, he opened the door and heard a hum of conversation coming from the sitting room. Taking a deep breath, he walked in and said, 'Hallo, everyone. Back at last.'

There was a stunned silence and Frank, who was about to pour Molly a drink, froze in mid gesture. She stared in wonder, and Cynthia went as white as a sheet. Only Roland and Doris regarded him calmly.

'Welcome back,' choked Frank, putting down the bottle and shaking his hand as if it was the village pump, while Molly rushed across the room and threw her arms around him.

'We've been so worried!' she cried. 'Even though Roland and Doris said you'd be back quite soon.'

'After we'd sorted out the fear-vampire, I came straight here to make sure Doris was safe,' said Roland. 'My boy, I'm desperately sorry for what I did.'

'The last time I saw you, Sir, you were fighting like a hero,' said Oliver, 'and I, for one, wouldn't be here without you.'

'You look so distinguished with that white hair, but more *complete,* more *vital,*' said Molly, a little apprehensively. 'And pleased to see me, I hope,' she added.

'More than I can say.'

'Where's Pierre?' said Cynthia. 'Please don't tell me he's dead.'

'Renewing an old acquaintance on the Shadow-side,' said Oliver. 'He'll be along when he's ready.'

'A good night's sleep for you now,' said Roland, 'and tomorrow we'll start preparing your case. If you'll allow me to assist you.'

Molly took Oliver's hand and said, 'Let's go home now, you can see Roland tomorrow.'

And he saw nothing wrong with that suggestion, although a good night's sleep wasn't what either of them had in mind.

***

221

The next morning when Oliver called round to the Chilvers' house, he found Roland waiting.

'Thanks for offering to help,' Oliver said. 'I assume you've had others like ours?'

'Most of the Inquiries I've handled were more complex,' Roland replied, rather put out, 'and go far beyond human understanding. Would a submission by a Planck-length species for enhanced quantum access mean anything to you, Oliver?'

'Sorry,' said Oliver. 'While we're waiting for the form to come, please tell me about what support we can get.'

'Before the Inquiry takes place,' said Roland, 'you may submit written evidence from up to three supporters, or nominate up to three to present evidence on the day.'

'Who should appear for us?' said Oliver.

'Your decision,' said Roland, 'but you must be careful about who you choose.'

'What about Pan? He'd be proof that a human from the real side can know and appreciate the Shadow-side.'

'I fear he'd have limited credibility,' said Roland. 'What did he show you of its great art collections, the music conservatoires, or the Athenian Agora? Would Arcadia project the right kind of *image* to support your case?'

'How about Brian?'

'His primary allegiance,' said Roland, 'like mine, will always be for the dominance on Earth of plant-based life. That might affect the tone of his submission, whatever the warmth he felt about you personally.'

'What about Meg and Myra?'

'Two of the most unclassifiable beings in creation,' said Roland.

'I see them as friends,' said Oliver.

'*You* might,' said Roland. 'Like most advanced beings, they're really *unreadable*. And therefore very unpredictable, like Lord Sebastian.'

'Yes, since I heard his preferred identity was an algorithm written on a cloud,' said Oliver, 'I've never taken him at face value.'

'Very wise,' said Roland, 'he's not remotely human.'

'What a trial this whole business has been!' said Oliver.

'Now *that's* a good line,' said Roland. 'You pursued this painful journey to the very end, without complaint. Really make them appreciate that!'

'I will!' said Oliver.

'And don't ignore the most important thing!' said Roland.

'You mean the portals, the dream-paths and 'realised' dream-matter on the Shadow-side? Humanity's unique gift to the galaxy.'

'Play that for all that its worth,' said Roland, 'always stressing that the unused dream-matter is disseminated by way of a deep relationship with the green realm of plants and trees.'

'You'd have me say that our greatest asset is a product of an intimate relationship with another species!' said Oliver.

'You have witnessed it with your own eyes,' said Roland. 'Human failure to recognise it does not diminish its importance. Is that the postman approaching?'

The most significant document in human history turned out to be a brown envelope, with Oliver's name wrongly spelt on the window.

'And a second-class stamp,' said Oliver. 'This isn't some kind of a *joke*, is it, Roland?'

'When I handled a case on the woodland scene,' said Roland, 'official messages would turn up in a scruffy nest full of bird shit.'

Inside the envelope was a poorly duplicated form, with a covering letter from the Galactic Inquiry Team Leader.

'Dear Sir/Madam/Other,' Oliver read, 'You are required to attend an Inquiry relating to your bid for human dominance on Solar Planet Three. On receipt of your application, the Inquiry will commence at 1000 Earth hours (GMT) at a time and a location to be advised. You may call up to three witnesses to support your case in person, OR submit up to three written submissions to the above address.'

'Let's look at the form,' said Roland.

'First it wants me to give my address, species, and how long I've been in my current state,' said Oliver. 'What does that mean?'

'Just put your age in Earth years,' said Roland. 'The 'current state' reference is to cover trans-species applicants. I take it you understand: 'State next of kin or nearest entity, dietary requirements and any allergies.'

'Are they serious?' Oliver said, scribbling an answer. 'And who should I put down to answer their question on sponsors?'

'I suggest,' said Roland, 'Lord Sebastian, Peer of the Celestial Realm, MA (Orion); Pan, Deity (Ancient). Dip. Leisure Studies. (Arcadia); and Lord Roland, Peer of the Green Mantle, author of 'Rooted to the Dark Spot' and 'Rhizone Rhapsody.''

'That last bit sounds like a book promotion!' said Oliver.

'And now the important sections,' said Roland briskly. 'Give brief details of the evolution of life on Earth and of your species.' I'm sure you can work that up by yourself.'

To the section asking for 'Degree of dominance sought,' Roland thought 'liberal' would be best, giving Oliver some leeway. He surmised that the Artificial bid would go for 'total,' which didn't give them much room for manoeuvre.

'Justification for the bid?' said Oliver.

'You need to emphasise the *potential* of humans to relate to other species, essential for effective leadership,' said Roland. 'So here you can describe your close relationship with a dog and several cats, first-hand knowledge of trees and shrubs, experience of hyphae and the micro-green realm, and friendship with a shrub-spirit, a cosmic were-cat and a trans-avian falcon.'

'Next section,' read Oliver. 'Special attributes possessed by the life-form seeking dominance.'

'The unique human ability to dream and *retain the best of that process in a permanent form* is the key point to make here,' said Roland, 'and add '*this ability will be made freely available to other galactic species, as mankind expands beyond its solar system.*''

'Sounds good, so far,' said Oliver.

'But not quite enough yet,' said Roland. 'You must also stress '*the reliance of the dream-world on the use of portals, and the de-toxification of the dream-matter by the Green Network.*'

'Wait a moment,' said Oliver, 'do I sense another *dilution* of the dominance bid for humanity?

'The rich advantages of a measure of joint control,' said Roland, 'would far outweigh the weakness of relying on a slight single bid.'

'Is our case that flimsy?'

'It's all relative,' said Roland. 'Look at what you're up against with the opposition. They may be ruthless and lack sensitivity to other life-forms, but they're efficient, consistent and effective. And that's good enough for some judges.'

'Whose side are you on, Roland?' said Oliver.

'I'm on the side of natural systems,' said Roland, 'and I believe that neither our plant-based nor your human approach alone would be a match for the opposition. But *together,* and bearing in mind we *already* work together to safeguard your best asset, we can prevail.'

'That only leaves a space for me to agree that the recommendation of the Inquiry will be final,' Oliver said, 'and no appeal is allowed.'

'Now I suggest you work up some response to the question about life on Earth,' said Roland, 'and look at the submission with your family and friends. It's your decision, but you know my view.'

'Yes,' said Oliver, with a grin, 'that's the one thing you have made clear!'

'And that, in a nutshell, is the position,' said Oliver that afternoon to the others, having outlined his journey and Roland's assessment of their bid.

'What an experience you've had,' said Frank, 'you lucky chap.'

'The idea of a partnership between mankind and the green realm sounds good to me,' said Molly.

'I agree,' said Cynthia. 'Little to lose and much to gain, for the good of the planet.'

'It would give your bid more weight,' added Frank.

'And risk the dominance of Earth by hostile *plant-like* creatures?' said Oliver.

'Triffids, rather than daffodils?' said Frank.

'I imagine we'll need some safeguards over that,' said Cynthia.

'I'm sure we'd get them from green supporters like Roland and Brian,' said Oliver, 'and remember, it works both ways in a partnership.'

The others agreed and the decision was taken, over a cup of coffee, for a joint bid, affecting the whole future of the human race.

Oliver and Roland then completed the form, attached to it supporting documents and confirmed they had no wish for nominations. It was then signed off as a joint bid, and sent by special courier to the specified address.

And, shortly afterwards, an e-mail arrived, asking them to take a hard copy of the enclosed Registration Form, which they must show to registration staff as proof of their invitation to the Inquiry, which would be held at the specified address in London three days later, at 10.00 am precisely.

18

'Are you sure this is the right place?' said Oliver to Roland, as they stood at the junction of Victoria Street and a small side-street. 'It can't be that scruffy building over there, surely?'

'I must say, I expected something rather more *dignified*,' said Roland when they walked over and read a tarnished brass sign on front of the building that said 'Inquiry Registration.'

'If it's where we have to go to save our entire species,' said Oliver, 'I suppose it doesn't really matter what it looks like.'

'Let's go and see,' said Roland.

They climbed the chipped front steps, pushed open a smeary plate-glass door, and passed into a vestibule, whose grubby walls were peeping out from behind peeling wallpaper. Dust covered every surface, and the smell of drains, disinfectant and cheap floor polish confirmed Oliver's foreboding about the place. This was further endorsed by the open counter of an office canteen on their right, manned by an adolescent skinhead, listlessly sliding cheeseburgers, greasy with rancid fat, around a large smoking hotplate.

In front of them they saw a notice on a rickety stand, with faded letters saying 'Reception' and an arrow pointing to the left. They turned the corner and walked along a dark corridor, the floor of which was covered with dirty carpeting, crisscrossed with black tape where it had ruptured. Oliver, dreading what he was going to find, pushed ahead towards an area where they could hear a hum of voices.

The over-heated hall they entered was crammed with a heaving mob jostling towards a wall on their right, punctuated at intervals by openings protected by grills. Behind them, sullen staff sat at cheap plastic counters, regarding the seething mass before them with cold indifference. Oliver and Roland joined a queue behind someone clutching a cage of birds, and another nursing a glass jar containing a stick insect, both with forms similar to theirs. Far ahead, at the head of the queue, they saw others being turned away or re-directed.

'Yes?' said the man when at last they reached his counter. He had a thin pencil moustache, smarmy, centrally parted hair and was cleaning his fingernails with what looked like a wet cotton bud.

'Dominance bid,' said Oliver, holding up the application.

'Single or other?' said the man, inspecting his nails with approval.

'Other,' said Roland.

'Room 14, down the corridor on the left. Next.'

After three more hours of queueing they were interviewed by an anorexic young woman with severe acne, and a pronounced facial tic.

'Dominance bid,' said Oliver, in reply to her question.

'Reference number?'

'1097,' said Oliver, having hastily scanned their application form.

'Does it say 'Pri' on it, or 'Fast Trk'?

Oliver looked at Roland, who consulted the form and said, 'It says 'Ord.'"

'And *this* says we only process 'Ords' on Wednesdays,' said the girl with a thin smile, pointing to a notice on the wall behind her. She then placed a card saying 'Closed' behind her grill.

Oliver, in despair, turned to Roland and said, 'Didn't you check our reference number?'

'Didn't need one last time.'

'When was that, in the middle ages?' said Oliver. 'Oh, what are we doing in this awful place!'

'Who knows?' said Roland, shrugging his shoulders.

'Let's get out, just for a moment,' said Oliver. 'I saw a lift on our way in, maybe we can get some fresh air on a higher floor.'

They pushed back through a throng of people and surprisingly found no-one by the lift doors, or even seeming to notice they were there. Oliver called the lift and when it came, the doors opened promptly. Once inside and alone, Roland pressed the button marked 'terrace,' but for some reason, they stopped several floors below on an unmarked level. Deciding to get out, they emerged into a spacious lobby bathed in soft light, illuminating a world of highly polished wood floors, designer rugs and original pictures. There was a subtle hint of sandalwood in the air, and expensive white leather armchairs neatly arranged around a sparkling glass coffee table. A slender jardinière holding an exquisite flower arrangement stood beside an elegant rosewood reception desk.

'Mr. Penrose and Lord Roland?' said a lovely, smart woman rising to greet them, and they both nodded. 'Please take a seat,' she said, pressing a button.

'Haven't we met somewhere before?' said Oliver, looking closely at her.

'Perhaps,' she said. *But where was it?* he wondered. His puzzlement grew.

After a few minutes Lord Sebastian came in to greet them, wearing a finely tailored grey suit, a snowy white shirt and a dazzling silk tie. With his shining silver hair and tanned face, he radiated bonhomie and good health. Shaking their hands warmly, he smiled and said, 'Good-day, gentlemen, here at last. We were getting a little worried.'

'We've been here for hours trying to register for the Inquiry,' said Oliver. 'We're happy to see you looking so well, Sir. When we last met you were going to war on the higher levels. And that was quite a fight, we heard.'

'Ah, how news travels,' Sebastian smiled. 'All water under the bridge now. But an ill wind as well, for I must confess to a small *promotion* after the fracas. Hardly worth the mention, a *tiny* elevation, but pleasing for one laboring so long in the vineyard.'

'Congratulations, Sir!' said Oliver, and Roland smiled broadly.

'Away with you – it's just a lot of stuff and nonsense,' said Sebastian. 'And now, gentlemen, how can I be of help to you?'

'Please help us register for our Inquiry,' said Roland.

'Not yet completed?' said Sebastian, looking vague.

'There are so many others downstairs,' said Oliver, 'all trying to be registered.'

'Downstairs?' said Sebastian. 'I don't follow you, there's no 'downstairs' here. Do you know anything about that, Estelle?'

'The time dilution control's been playing up, my Lord,' she said. 'The man they sent said he'd fixed it. It's been flickering on and off since he went.'

'Ah, it sounds as if they got caught up in an Open Day. How frightful. Near or far future, Estelle?'

'Near, my Lord.'

'Everyone wanting to run things their way, I suppose.'

'I'm afraid so.'

'Lord Sebastian, may we ask your people to handle our application?' said Oliver.

'Always happy to help people like you,' he replied, 'not like that Open Day rabble down there, 'entitled' by a new breed of leftie-leaning galactic controllers, with their 'inclusive' stellar policies. Free dominance bids for all species, self-declarers, the lot. Drones waking up thinking they're queen bees, and getting a hive allowance!'

Estelle snipped off an exquisite bloom from the flower arrangement and carefully arranged it in his buttonhole, and he beamed and calmed down.

'May I ask what brings you here, my Lord?' said Oliver.

'When we heard you'd be registering here today, Estelle found us this office suite,' Sebastian said. 'We sent word to you to come here and clearly it didn't reach you. But you were *inclined* to take the lift, so here you are!'

'And very welcome,' said Estelle, smiling.

'I still feel we've met before,' said Oliver, 'but where?'

'Perhaps it was at the Grand Hotel after your first transit,' said Sebastian. 'How long ago that must seem to you!'

'Yes, indeed,' said Oliver, 'how nice to see you again, Estelle. May I introduce to you Lord Roland, my friend and helper.'

'Welcome, my Lord,' said Estelle. 'Many congratulations on your elevation to the galactic peerage. Who would have thought when we first met that you would become so important, you with only the one planet to look after, and that in winter. I seem to remember you married little Doris; some kind of library assistant, was she not? A nice, homely girl, from some remote location, as I recall? In the Kuiper belt, or was it the Oort Cloud?'

'Ah, er, well,' stammered Roland, looking at their host for support.

'Lord Sebastian, do you know who's chairing the Inquiry?' said Oliver.

'Not at present,' said Sebastian, 'but Estelle may enlighten you when she registers your bid. And now I fear I must to Ganymede Two for several millennia of their years, which, I fear, will seem to me as long as if they were terrestrial. Back for tea. Estelle will look after you whilst I'm away.'

***

Estelle, who seemed quietly amused at Roland's discomfort, led them to an adjacent office to wait, and when they sat down Oliver asked her how long she'd worked with Lord Sebastian.

'Since I left the Galactic Temping Agency,' she smiled. 'It seems light-years ago.'

'What was he like when you first worked with him?' said Oliver. 'He once told me he preferred looking like an algorithm written on a cloud.'

'Before my time,' she said, 'and certainly not for several millennia. At present he favours an *organic* rather than an abstract form, for many stellar systems are currently dominated by Artificial Intelligence, and he doesn't wish to be seen to support such cultures.'

'What about you, Estelle?' asked Oliver. 'Do you have a home planet, and other forms, too?'

'I come from a beautiful nebula your astronomers call 'little Gem,'' she said, 'it's in the constellation Sagittarius. As for my form, I can assume any shape I choose. Lord Sebastian likes that, for mature entities like him grow weary of change, but relish variety in familiar objects.'

'Is he very powerful?'

'Immensely, judged by human standards,' said Estelle, 'but relative to others, who knows? He's really quite sweet, and so pleased that, at last, he's been awarded a black hole pass, in perpetuity. It gives him instant universe-wide access, only the one cosmos of course, but that's all he's ever wanted. And I'm a one-universe girl, too. Isn't that lucky!'

She broke off, for the pad she was carrying had begun glowing. 'There's a message coming through on ethereal mail,' she said, 'advising us that the Inquiry will convene in Committee Room 6.'

'What should we do now, Estelle?' said Oliver.

'Wait here for his Lordship to come back,' she smiled, 'and I'll arrange for you to have refreshments. Good seeing you again, Rolly. *Library* assistant, ha!'

'What did she mean by that?' said Oliver.

'Her idea of a joke, I imagine,' said Roland, 'and a pretty poor one at that.'

***

When Lord Sebastian appeared later, he said, 'I understand you know the date and time of your Inquiry, gentlemen.'

'Yes,' said Oliver, 'time's a bit tight, but we'll manage.'

'Ah, *timing*,' said Sebastian, 'such a *variable* as your esteemed Einstein discovered.'

'It's been postponed!' Oliver cried.

'Or cancelled,' added Roland.

'Neither,' said Sebastian. 'The excellent news is that you've been fast-tracked, in what I can only describe as a *lumber* operation: clearing a log-jam of submissions and a back-log of cases.'

'When is it to be?' said Oliver, grimly.

'Two o'clock this afternoon.'

Oliver's stomach gave a lurch. 'We *can't* be ready by then!' he cried, sitting down with his head in his hands. He felt like weeping.

'There is a little more,' Sebastian said, easing his collar with his index finger, 'hardly worth the mention.'

'More?' said Roland, suddenly alert.

'Today, what's left of it, has been designated an 'Open Half-Day,'' said Sebastian, 'to 'demonstrate the optimum use of scarce resources as part of a visible democratic process.' I suppose that means something to someone or other.'

'And we're still expected to make our case with that going on!' screeched Oliver.

'So it would seem,' said Sebastian, mildly. 'Perhaps some gentle *jostling* to go with the infectious chanting, but what an opportunity to display the indomitability of the human spirit!'

'How can the Inquiry do justice to our case in that time?' cried Oliver.

'Ah, here comes Estelle with some drinks,' said Sebastian, 'and after a toast to your undoubted success, she'll find you somewhere quiet to prepare for what lies ahead.'

***

After Estelle had found them a small office adjacent to the reception area, Oliver and Roland sat down and reviewed the position.

'We haven't much time before the Inquiry,' said Oliver. 'Shall we run through our submission one last time?'

'Nothing else to do,' said Roland. 'I'd better ring Doris and tell her what's happening.' And when he'd finished giving her the news, he asked casually if she remembered someone from the past called Estelle.

'You mean that tart of a morph who infatuated you pathetic men so much,' snapped Doris. 'Why? Have you run across her?'

'Just met someone who reminded me of her,' said Roland. 'Not important.'

'Not what you said last time,' said Doris, her lips tightly pursed. 'Don't expect me to wait up for you!'

***

Oliver and Roland discussed their efforts with Lord Sebastian, who had popped in, doubtless from some distant part of the galaxy, to see how they were faring. When they had run through the material, Oliver turned to Sebastian and said, 'Well, that's the best we can do.' He was feeling curiously light-hearted now that all hope had gone.

'It has a rare ring of *authenticity* about it,' said Sebastian, 'so appealing, and not common, even at Inquiries. I could quote instances…'

'Forgive me,' said Oliver, 'but do you know who's presiding at the Inquiry?'

'We're in luck,' said Sebastian, 'he's youngish, galaxy educated and from a rocky planet in Pegasus. We may address him as 'Judge Fortify' – they only have numbers on his world. At home he's four-two-five.'

'Has he had *any* time to become familiar with our submission?' said Oliver.

'Several of your earth years, if he needed them,' said Sebastian. 'Always remember that time, so elusive to the hasty grasp, if well-handled can be fashioned to fit most needs.'

'So he may have sought advice from others?' said Roland.

'Oh yes. And Earth-biased, all of them, I'll be bound,' said Sebastian. 'Keep it local, it's the *modern* way.'

'May we see their comments?' said Oliver.

'Afraid not,' said Sebastian, 'submissions are never available to an applicant.'

'Can we know who they are?'

'Not possible,' said Sebastian. 'Anyhow, it's who they *were*, because they're usually deceased.'

'*Deceased!* If they were *dead,* how could they submit anything?'

'You've got a Shadow-side, haven't you?' said Sebastian. 'Full to the brim with wonderful persons and characters from the pick of the very best human dreams.'

'And all *wholesome,*' put in Roland, 'thanks to the green realm.'

'Sounds *ghoulish,*' said Oliver. 'So which of these dead souls might have been approached?'

'Anyone thought 'suitable and available,'' said Sebastian, 'any fictional character or person of note being the subject of dreams and allowed by the Dream-Masters to be 'realised' on the Shadow-side."

'So it might have been Plato or Aristotle?' said Oliver.

'Unlikely in our case,' said Sebastian, 'everyone wants them.'

'Who else, then?' said Oliver.

'I'd guess scientists, and at your level more Hawkins than Huxley, and Dirac than Darwin,' said Sebastian. 'You can forget the really big hitters like Newton and Einstein, but you may have had a look in with Jenner or Descartes, as they're out of fashion.'

'Is that all?' smiled Oliver.

'And the 'Man on the Clapham Space-shuttle,'' said Lord Sebastian, 'you'll have to explain that one to me.'

'Later,' said Oliver, wearily, 'now it's time to go. How do we get to the room where the Inquiry's being held?'

'Lift down to ground level, through the hall on the left,' said Sebastian, 'and then go along the corridor, and you'll find Committee Room 6 on the left. You can wait there. Good luck.'

***

Committee Room 6 was spartan. On the floor, the thin lino had split in places, showing the dusty concrete beneath. Damaged tubular steel chairs were stacked in one corner, partially covered by a filthy curtain that had long parted from its wall fittings. A plain wooden bench faced a cheap plywood desk, its scratched surface bearing the rings of countless mugs, ink-stains and graffiti. On one wall a map of the world showed the countries of the British empire in faded red, and on the other there was a picture of the Queen when she was a young woman. The room's redeeming features were its remote location and a sturdy door, eliminating the clamour of the 'entitled' thronging the public areas.

When Oliver and Roland arrived, a pale-faced adolescent with unavoidable acne but wholly preventable tattooing was sitting on a bench in front of the desk, wearing a baseball cap on backwards, with the words 'Make Artials Great Agane' written on it. Sitting next to him was a very thin man with scanty facial hair and pebble glasses, wearing a greasy anorak two sizes too big for him, and holding a kilner jar full of ants. The rest of the form was occupied by a large, odoriferous woman, with a weather-beaten face and matching moustache, wearing a dirty tweed skirt and a Barbour jacket in the last stages of disintegration. None of them glanced up as Oliver and Roland came in and sat down.

After a few minutes the door opened, and a gust of cheap scent announced the arrival of a bulky, heavily made-up woman, plump feet squeezed into high-heeled, patent leather pumps, and wearing an academic gown. She counted the applicants, nodding her head as she glanced at each person. She then announced that the Inquiry was in session, with His Celestial Honour Judge Fortify presiding, and the applicants should rise. Stepping back, she bowed as he walked past her clad in a scarlet robe.

Motioning the audience to sit, Fortify, a cheerful, round-faced, totally bald, human lookalike, sat down on a throne-like chair behind the desk and regarded them in silence for a few moments. Then, in a soft, friendly voice he thanked them for attending at such short notice and assured them that their submissions had been scrutinised with the greatest care. After that he turned to the usher, and whispered something in her ear. She crossed the room and spoke softly to the man with the ants and the doggy woman, who stood up, bowed and left the court.

'Thank you, Madam usher,' said the Judge, who turned to the remaining applicants, shaking his head, and murmuring, 'De minimus non curat lex.'

'What's that mean?' whispered Oliver to Roland.

'The law does not concern itself with trifles,' he replied quietly.

'Silence in court!' roared the usher, glaring at him.

The Judge then donned a pair of half-moon glasses, opened the folder on his desk, and regarded it for a moment, before addressing the room. 'Your submissions have concerned issues for which a large body of Galactic Law exists,' he said, 'and to which I have been able to refer for guidance. But few cases are without unique features, and I invite each party to add to their submission if they wish. Then I will retire to consider my verdict, which will be presented to you, without delay, or any opportunity for appeal.'

He looked at the AI representative, smiled and asked him to go first.

'An AI planet, like, well-led and efficient,' mumbled the youth, 'would likely safeguard its resources rather than mal-use and well-waste super-irreplaceable terrestrial stuff. Bionic stuff is kinda super-awesome, and, like, the resulting super-organisms, can well replace the flawed natural shit. Then the mal-stuff of bigman would like come to an end, well benefitting the planet, and all its natural shit.'

'Thank you,' said the Judge. 'And the Joint Case?'

'I am confident that my experiences with non-human life-forms on Earth,' said Oliver, 'demonstrate that humans, like me, have the potential to understand and then care for other species. As custodian of the planet, we can also offer the galaxy the unique gift of our ability to 'dream-realise,' preserving the choicest fruits of this process via a network of unique portals and natural channels. And, in partnership with our green kin, a healthy, progressive future for the planet is really possible.'

'Thank you, everyone,' said the Judge, 'I will take your words into consideration.'

'All rise,' said the usher, and they all stood as he took his leave.

Oliver smiled at the AI representative, and wished him well as he passed by him on the way out.

'Fuckin' bunch of wankers,' replied the youth, chewing and giving him a rude finger gesture. 'Got 'losers', like, well-wrote all over you.'

***

In an hour Judge Fortify returned and addressed the court. 'Applicants will be interested to know that a recent Cosmic Ruling designated the light matter planet known as Earth to be a 'Site of Stellar Significance.' This automatically protects its Shadow-side twin, with its artifacts and creatures, and safeguards the network of portals connecting the two planets.'

'We're home and dry,' whispered Roland to Oliver.

'And although I commend the *nature* of the joint submission,' the Judge continued, 'it failed to persuade me that the human race has the capacity to evolve, *in a timely fashion*, in a way that protects existing planetary assets, even with the help of its green colleagues.'

'After all our hard work,' said Oliver, bitterly.

'Neither do I feel that AI dominance is, at present, in Earth's best interests,' the Judge continued, 'either in the light of the current submission, or in view of the evidence available from other planets.'

'However, in the longer term, it is felt that the planet will benefit from a true marriage of the natural with the artificial, in the interest of its natural life-forms as well as its own physical wellbeing. An interim arrangement is therefore proposed, which will safeguard natural life on Earth whilst limiting the unrestricted development of AI. This 'breathing space' is intended to enable a strategic plan to be developed, agreed by all Earth parties, with a view to obtaining Galactic Approval.'

'How?' breathed Oliver.

'I consider that the way to achieve this,' continued the Judge, 'is through wise direction and stewardship, and I direct the Lord Sebastian to carry out such a task, showing bias to neither party represented here today, or any other. A further Inquiry will convene when the work nears its conclusion, to consider its recommendations in line with the court's current thinking.'

He rose, everyone stood and, when he'd left the room, Oliver turned to Roland, and said, 'The crafty old devil, I'll bet he knew it all along. Let's go and have it out with him.'

***

'Ah, you've caught me,' said Lord Sebastian. 'Estelle has cleared up here, and we were just *running* along. Everything *satisfactory,* I hope.'

'Did you know from the very start this was going to happen?' said Oliver.

'Got me there, gentlemen,' said Sebastian. 'Oddly enough, only a moment ago, the same question was put to me by your opposition.'

'And what do we do now?' cried Oliver.

'There I can help you, my dear fellow,' said Lord Sebastian.

'How?'

'I'll ask old Horace to take you back in time, and by changing a few little things, you'll forget everything that's happened. Easy when you know how.'

'What sort of 'little things?''

'Oh, I don't know – talking to animals, seeing how trees live, meeting different creatures, things like that,' said Lord Sebastian. 'Horace's good at smoothing over Father Time…talking of which…'

'What about me?' said Roland.

'Ah, now, of course, not being human, you're rather *different*,' said Sebastian, 'and, when all's said and done, you're undeniably a *celestial* being. One with a bright future too, with the little promotion I have in mind. Actually, not so little…'

'What can I say… you didn't have to… thanks very much,' muttered Roland, not looking at Oliver.

'Well, if it's the only way,' said Oliver, thinking how nice it would be to see Molly.

'Tell you what,' said Sebastian, 'when you see Horace, tell him I said you could both choose one thing from your journey to keep in your new life. That goes for you too, Roland. Must dash now, all good wishes. Come along, Estelle.'

EPILOGUE

It was when Frank was driving his brother home from the south coast that Oliver suggested he should take over the wheel for the next stretch of the journey. Frank agreed, and at the next lay-by he turned off and drew up behind a large black van, which pulled away as he parked. They were crossing in front of their car to change places when he spotted something moving in the road, near where the van had been standing.

'Oliver,' he said, 'they've driven off and left something on the road, which I think I saw move.' Walking over to see what it was, he hesitated for a moment, but relaxed when he saw it was a puppy. He picked up the tiny creature, but as he did so he saw a cheerful young man running towards him, and noticed that the van had stopped some way up the road.

'Sorry to trouble you,' said the man, 'we nearly left the little blighter behind. Come on, you!' he said, retrieving the puppy. Cradling the small creature in his arms, he thanked Frank and walked back to his van. When it had driven off, the brothers looked at each other and shrugged. But just before they left, Frank saw a movement in a tree above them, and thought it just might be a peregrine falcon.

Oliver looked up at the lovely hawk and, for some strange reason, felt a yearning in his heart, and a lump coming into his throat. On reaching home he was amazed to see another falcon (surely not the same bird) perched high on a tree in the garden and found himself calling to it in a strangely familiar way. And when it swooped down onto his outstretched arm and looked at him, head on one side, he was speechless with happiness. And after that first meeting, the lovely, silent bird never failed to answer his call, and neither did his wonder at its behaviour and beauty, or joy at its return.

***

Shortly after the hawk appeared, when Frank and Oliver were having a quiet evening drink, Frank suddenly said, 'I think Roland's got a girlfriend.'

'Never,' said Oliver, 'he's not the type. Anyway with Doris around...'

'Every few weeks when his wife visits her sister,' said Frank, 'I'm sure I've glimpsed a young woman next door. Doris won't be there tonight, so why don't you go and say hallo to Roland, who you haven't seen for a while. I'm sure he'll ask you in for a moment, and you can look around.'

'You wish me to *spy* on your friend, and your neighbour,' said Oliver. 'What do you take me for?'

Frank told him, and Oliver went next door at the double, and knocked on the door.

'Just thought I'd say hallo,' he said, when after a pause, Roland opened the door.

'Good to see you,' said Roland, clearly pre-occupied. 'I'm pleased you came because I wanted to let you and the others know we're leaving. An opportunity's come up and we're moving away, very shortly. As he spoke a ravishingly beautiful woman came down the stairs and smiled at Oliver.

'Oh, by the way, this is my niece,' said Roland.

'How do you do?' she said to Oliver, extending her hand.

Her hand felt cool and soft, and his heart gave a little leap.

'Hello,' he said, looking closely at her. 'Haven't we met before?'

'I don't think so,' she said. 'My name's Estelle.'

Oliver was certain they'd met and spent the next two days trying to think when and where. He needn't have bothered, for shortly afterwards Roland and Doris left the area, without even saying goodbye or leaving a forwarding address.

However, some weeks later, when Oliver was walking alone across the downs and musing about their sudden departure, his thoughts turned to the beautiful woman he'd met that night. And then, like the faintest trace of a beguiling perfume, his mind was touched with a tender, inexplicable longing, a sad-sweet feeling, so elusive that he stopped in his tracks to focus on its source. But before it drifted away, he could have sworn he heard the faintest murmur of a sweet voice saying, 'I'm a one-universe girl, isn't that lucky?' But even before the thought had fled away and he'd forgotten it, he couldn't fathom out what it meant.

***

And thereafter Oliver went on to lead a full, active and, on the whole, happy life. He also acquired a love of poetry, especially that relating to nature, but was untroubled by the stirring of any long-forgotten memory, or clues to his 'dream-journey' stimulated by the work of poets and visionaries. So he never lamented the 'music that was fled,' or asked 'where is it now, the glory and the dream,' or wondered whether we are such 'stuff as dreams are made on', or thought deeply about what Romeo meant speaking about 'dreaming things true.'

But when he was very old, the last of the group and lonely, thumbing through a family Bible, he chanced upon a passage concerning the last days, which included the lines: 'your young men shall see visions, and your old men will dream dreams.' And that made him sad and resigned, for increasingly he felt himself to be in a world no longer a 'country for old men.' And that, in the end, and in the absence of love, the only things worth living for were dreams.

He sighed, and then after calling out goodbye to his beloved wife Molly, dead now for two years, but in his faltering mind still resting upstairs, frail and bed-ridden, where he'd faithfully cared for her, he left the house for his usual walk on the downs. He took his walking stick from its usual place, called to his hawk, who swooped down and perched silently on his outstretched arm, and together they went quietly on their way, as they had for so many years.

But this time the walk was different, for as he trudged uphill, along the well-known track, the hawk spoke to him for the first time. 'Walk towards Dragon Hill, Master,' he said, 'only a few steps more than usual, and then, as I am, I must leave you. But soon, as I will be, we will be together.'

As Oliver faltered uphill, his breath rasping and weak, he thought he saw figures ahead. He shook his head as if to clear away the mist fogging his sight, but they were still there: Meg and Myra, Brian and Roland, Pan and Wedros. And Lord Sebastian, smiling and holding out his arms, and with him his dearest Molly, Frank and Cynthia beside her, and next to them a handsome dog and a fine cat.

***

He was quite dead when the gentle walker found him lying there on the Ridgeway with a quiet smile on his face. And beside him was the body of a bird, which the man knew was a peregrine falcon. And that puzzled him, for it was rare to find one there. But not unheard of, unlike the great white-tailed eagle, riding the air currents high above him. Entranced, he watched as it circled up and up, before swooping down, dipping out of sight beyond the nearby hill. And although the walker returned, time and again, hoping to catch another glimpse of the majestic bird sweeping down on huge wings from high above before wheeling away over the hill, as if responding to some familiar call, he never did.